THE PENITENT GUN

AN EZEKIEL FLAGG WESTERN

THE PENITENT GUN

ROD TIMANUS

THORNDIKE PRESS
A part of Gale, a Cengage Company

GALE
A Cengage Company

GALE
A Cengage Company

Thorndike Press® Large Print Hardcover Western.
The text of this Large Print edition is unabridged.
Other aspects of the book may vary from the original edition.
Set in 16 pt. Plantin.

LIBRARY OF CONGRESS CIP DATA ON FILE.
CATALOGUING IN PUBLICATION FOR THIS BOOK
IS AVAILABLE FROM THE LIBRARY OF CONGRESS.

ISBN-13: 979-8-88578-175-6 (hardcover alk. paper)

Published in 2023 by arrangement with Rod Timanus

Printed in Mexico
Print Number: 1   Print Year: 2023

THE PENITENT GUN

CHAPTER 1

"I never knew Ezekiel Flagg, the killer of men. He was a former lawman, an Indian scout, and a bounty hunter. Being just a wisp of a boy when I was told of his fearsome reputation, I was both fascinated and appalled by what I heard. I did know Zeke Smith, the hired hand, and he was my friend."

—From the journal of
William "Willie" Stevens

It was a typical spring day in the Red Rock Country of Arizona Territory. The mornings were cold, the air so crisp it seemed to crackle with every steamy exhaled breath. By mid-morning, however, the welcome warmth of the sun was so intense that coats, jackets, and scarves were of no further use and were gratefully removed. Eleven-year-old Willie Stevens, still clad in his heavy coat and cap against the chill, was carrying an armload of wood he had chopped earlier that morning into the house for the cook-stove. He stopped in mid-stride when he noticed a lone figure astride a mule on the road approaching their front gate.

"Nana?" Willie called out toward the chicken coop beside the barn. "Somebody's coming!"

The wizened old woman who emerged from the coop, shutting the door behind her so no chickens escaped, was bent and weathered by the harsh life she had lived. She walked with a slight limp from an old leg injury that had not healed properly, clutching the wicker basket she had filled with eggs tight to her chest. Wisps of white hair peeked out from beneath the shawl she wore over her head. She stopped beside Willie, staring intently at the approaching stranger.

"Best go fetch your ma," she murmured.

Willie dropped his armload of wood and bounded up the two porch stairs to the front door of the house. Just as he reached for the latch, the door flew open, and Willie's mother stepped out, shotgun in hand. They nearly collided in the doorway. Nana was already hobbling toward the gate as the stranger dismounted and stood awaiting her arrival. Standing beside his mother on the

8

porch, shotgun cradled in her arms like a newborn, Willie saw the stranger do something he had never seen another man do when speaking to his mother or grandmother. He removed his hat. Nana and the stranger stood talking for a few minutes, and then she unlatched the gate to let him in.

The two approached the house, the stranger adjusting his pace to Nana's and leading his mule by the reins. He and Nana exchanged a few words, and then he reached out and took the basket of eggs from her with his free hand. Nana laughed, and her step seemed to lighten a bit. When they stopped in front of the porch, Willie noticed the stranger's mule was alert to its new surroundings, head and ears raised, eyes darting about, and nostrils flared wide to inhale new scents. Somehow, he thought the stranger was taking it all in, too.

"This fellow is looking for work," Nana said as she retrieved the basket of eggs. "Mr. Schneider at the mercantile sent him."

As before, the stranger pulled off his slouch hat, exposing a mop of sandy-colored hair streaked with a bit of white that must have been combed at one time, and smiled up at Willie's mother.

"The name's Smith, Zeke Smith, ma'am,

and I could surely use some employment." His voice was mellow, not especially deep in tone, but nonetheless commanded attention.

"I'm Rebecca Stevens," Willie's mother replied, brushing a few stray strands of blonde hair from her face that had escaped being tied off at the nape of her neck. "You say Mr. Schneider sent you?"

"Yes, ma'am. He didn't need a clerk or stockman when I asked, but he said you might need some help out here. Looking around, I can see your front fence could use some shoring up, the house roof is missing a few shingles, and the chicken coop door could be rehinged. I imagine I could find enough chores to keep me busy."

"What sort of wages would you expect, Mr. Smith?"

"Just Zeke, ma'am, I prefer just Zeke. All I need is a cozy place in the barn for me and my mule, and a nightly home-cooked meal if you can spare the vittles. If you set it out on the porch, I'll collect it up and dine in the barn."

While Zeke and his mother talked, Willie was busy studying the man. Zeke Smith was of medium height, lean but not skinny. His face sported the stubble of a white beard and was not nearly as wrinkled as Nana's but still showed the furrows of age and exposure to the elements. His eyes were pale blue, like the reflection of the sky off an icy pond in the dead of winter. His clothing showed the wear of long use at the elbows and knees. His gun belt was old and weathered, the holster worn in a cross-draw position on his left side, and the grips of the Colt .45 in that holster appeared smooth and well cared for.

"Willie?" His mother's voice tugged him from his silent observations.

"Yes, Ma?"

"Show Zeke to the barn so he can find the cozy place he requires for himself and his mule. Then come wash up for breakfast."

Willie did as he was told. Walking toward the barn, he was surprised when Zeke casually asked, "Is that your father up on the hill behind the house?"

"My father? Yes . . . he's there . . ." Willie glanced up toward the little hill and the rough-hewn marker that stood beneath an ancient pine tree.

Without looking at Willie, Zeke continued to speak, as if he were thinking out loud. "That's where I would want to be, watching over the family."

"Do you have any family, Zeke?" Willie asked.

"No."

Something about Zeke's face suggested that might be a painful subject. Willie said, "Your mule looks sturdy. What's his name?"

Zeke smiled. "*Her* name is Mule, but she doesn't pull loads. She's my transport and will take me anywhere I wish without complaint."

They reached the barn. Willie pulled open the door, and they went in. The interior was cool, dark, and musky smelling. They stood just inside the door while their eyes adjusted to the light difference. Off to the right, an old mare named Molly nickered in her stall, and Zeke's mule answered with a low bray. There were six stalls in the barn, three on each side, but only Molly's was occupied. A small hayloft up above was half full of bales, and at the back end of the building were two doors that led to rooms on either side of another barn door smaller than the one through which they had entered. Shafts of sunlight pierced the darkness through gaps in the exterior wall boards and flooded in through small windows in each of the stalls.

"The two rooms down at the end are a tool room and a tack and feed room," Willie said as they walked down the center aisle. "You can clean out one of them — there isn't much of anything in either one — and stay in there if you want. They each have a window that looks out over the corral in back."

"I'll just bed down in an empty stall," Zeke replied. "Looks like there would be more elbow room."

As they passed by Molly's stall, she reacted to the strange scent of the newcomers and kicked the wall with a hind leg. Willie watched, amazed, as Zeke's head snapped around toward the unexpected noise, his knees bending slightly and his right hand flying to his pistol. Apparently realizing that Willie had noticed his reaction, Zeke chuckled and let his hand drop. "Well, now it appears I have to get used to a whole new set of regular sounds. Shouldn't take too long."

He stopped at the stall beside the one opposite Molly's and began to unload his gear from his mule, tossing his bedroll, a bulging carpetbag, and saddlebags into the corner and dropping a bag of feed grain on the floor outside. Then he set about uncinching and removing the saddle and blanket, which he placed on the floor beside the bag of grain.

After leading the mule into the stall next to the one where he had stowed his gear, he removed the bridle and reins and then stepped back out, swinging the stall gate closed behind him. The mule draped its head over the gate and stared across the aisle at Molly, who had turned in her own stall to look back in the same manner.

"Now the girls can get to know each other," Zeke said. "I'll finish putting my gear away properly later. Right now, your ma promised me a cup of strong, hot coffee while you folks have breakfast, and I need to get to the house to collect it before it gets cold."

CHAPTER 2

"Zeke told me to always be aware of my surroundings because you never know when you'll have to dodge out of the way of a stampede."

Willie lay in his bed up in the half loft of the house listening to his mother and grandmother talking down below at the kitchen table after the dinner dishes had been cleared and washed. He usually didn't eavesdrop on their conversations as they sewed or knitted at night; in fact the sound of their voices always lulled him to sleep. But he knew who they were talking about. Zeke had been with them a week and had proved himself an able worker, up before the sun and busy with some chore by first light. He sometimes helped Willie chop wood or carry the basket of collected eggs for Nana, but mostly he worked on the heavier tasks that needed to be done.

15

Nana's voice drifted up to him on the warm air from the kitchen and fireplace. "All I'm saying is, he is respectful and quiet. We should consider allowing him to take his meals in the house with us."

"That would be up to him," Ma replied. "Perhaps he prefers to be alone, but you can make the offer."

"Have you noticed that he always returns his plate, utensils, and cup rinsed off? That shows a proper upbringing," Nana continued.

Ma chuckled. "Yet you wash them again."

"No man can ever wash dishes properly," Nana replied with mock haughtiness.

Willie smiled when he heard his mother laugh at Nana's remark. It was a lilting, joyous sound she had not made since the death of her husband, his father, and it warmed his heart to hear it again. His eyelids were heavy now, and he could no longer keep them open. The last sound he heard was the boards, nailed to the roof rafters as a rough ceiling for the loft, creaking from temperature change as the heat rising from below collected above him and warmed the undersides of the wood cooled by the outside air.

The next morning his mother had to climb

halfway up the ladder to the loft to rouse Willie from his slumber. He woke to her voice calling his name and stirred under the covers. Groggy from staying awake later than he should have, he sat up. She bade him good morning and eased back down the ladder as Willie stumbled out of bed and began to dress.

Later, after the morning chores were done, Willie sat at the kitchen table with his mother doing his assigned lessons in reading, writing, and figures she insisted on teaching him every day because there was no school in the area. A gentle knock sounded at the door, and she rose to answer it. Zeke stood on the porch, hat in hand. "Just thought I would tell you I'm starting on the front fence, ma'am, but the shovel handle is about to give up the ghost and will need to be replaced soon. The axe handle is about ready to crack, too. If it does, it could hurt the boy while he's chopping wood."

"Thank you, Zeke," she replied. "I'll add those to the list of supplies we need for our next trip into town in a few days."

As Zeke turned to leave, Willie leapt from his chair and rushed to the door. "I'm finished with my lessons, Ma, can I go help Zeke?"

"As long as you are a help and not a bother," she answered with a smile.

"He's no bother," Zeke said. "I enjoy his company."

They stepped outside, and Zeke retrieved the tools from where he'd left them by the porch steps. As the two walked down to the front fence, Zeke handed Willie the shovel to carry while he carried a pick, digging bar, and a bucket of water. When they reached the fence, Zeke stood and stared for a minute at a stand of evergreen trees several hundred feet distant from the road. Just as Willie was about to ask him what was wrong, Zeke started moving down the line of fence posts, shaking each one to see how loose they were. Willie noticed a pile of new posts nearby in the tall grass, along with a hammer and canvas bag of nails, obviously brought down earlier in preparation for the day's task. He noted also Zeke's gun belt atop the pile, neatly wrapped around the holster.

Within an hour their coats came off in the morning heat, and they had found seven loose posts along the fence line, three of which felt as if the bottoms had rotted away. As Zeke loosened the soil around them with the digging bar, Willie scoured the area for rocks to place in the holes they would dig around the new posts to stop the wood from wobbling.

"Hot," Zeke muttered as he slid his suspender straps off his shoulders and pulled off his sweat-soaked shirt. Willie stared, open mouthed, at the scars covering the man's upper torso that showed white against his tanned skin. There were two long welts across his back that appeared to have healed up and several large, roundish indented scars down to his waist. Across his chest and stomach there were more long scars that could have been from deep cuts and numerous indents like the ones on his back, only smaller. Both his arms were covered with similar healed wounds.

Zeke half turned toward him then, and Willie dropped his gaze to the dirt. It was rude to stare like that, but, fortunately, Zeke didn't seem to have noticed. He had dug out around three of the loose fence posts and started on a fourth. When he was done with that, he pulled the old, rotting posts out and replaced each of them with a new post, holding them upright while Willie followed along dropping rocks into the holes and pushing the dirt back in with his hands.

They were still hard at work when Nana approached them, carrying her wicker basket. "Fresh baked biscuits, boys," she called out to them. Zeke scrambled to retrieve his shirt from the fence board where he'd draped it and hurriedly pulled it on.

Nana chuckled as she drew close. "No need for modesty, I've seen plenty of bare chests before. Besides that, even if I were twenty years younger, I'd still be too old for you." She handed the basket to Willie.

Zeke laughed as Willie dug in, pulling aside the cloth that was keeping the biscuits warm and grabbing one. Willie handed it to Zeke and snatched up another for himself. As Zeke chewed a mouthful of warm biscuit he leaned toward Nana and quietly asked, "You have neighbors hereabouts?"

Nana waved toward the evergreen trees that had caught Zeke's attention earlier. "Mr. Beecher lives a few miles away over yonder. He brings us smoked venison and turkey after he feeds his family and delivers hay for us to put up for the winter. In return we let him help himself to our apple orchard in season. Why do you ask?"

"I remember passing his place on the way here," Zeke mused. "I thought I saw someone in the woods out there. It could have been your neighbor out hunting."

"Probably was," Nana agreed. "There's Apaches hereabouts, but we haven't had any trouble with them for a while." Her face clouded. "Not since they killed my son two years back."

"Sorry to hear that," Zeke replied. "What happened?"

"A homestead further down the road was raided and burned out, the young couple living there killed," Nana said. "The marshal got up a posse to go after the raiders, and my son went along. We heard later the Apaches turned back and ambushed them. There was a fight, and my son was shot dead. His name was William. Willie is named after him."

Listening to the story Willie felt a hollow pain in his stomach, and tears welled up in his eyes. Zeke gently placed a hand on the boy's shoulder.

"Let's get back to work," he said. Willie was happy to comply.

As Nana turned to leave, she said, "We would be pleased if you would join us in the house for supper tonight, Zeke. We have to be better dining companions than a horse and a mule."

Zeke smiled as he picked up the digging bar again. "I would be delighted."

He began to dig around the base of the next fence post that needed replacing, softly whistling a jaunty tune. Willie, back at his job of gathering rocks and stones to secure

21

the fence post, was glad Zeke seemed so happy at the prospect of sharing supper with them that night.

CHAPTER 3

"We all have a past. It follows us like a shadow that we can never escape and can only come to terms with in the present."

That evening, as grey clouds scudded across the darkening sky on a cold north wind, Willie's mother sent him out to the barn to tell Zeke the evening meal was cooked and ready. Zeke was already approaching the house from the barn, and they met halfway between the two buildings. He was wearing a clean white shirt and black pants that still showed the creases where they had been neatly folded and a bright yellow bandanna tied around his neck. He was not wearing his ever-present pistol belt. But what struck the boy most about his appearance was his clean-shaven face and neatly trimmed moustache.

"You shaved!" Willie exclaimed.

"I haven't forgotten how," Zeke replied

with a grin as he gingerly wiped away a bead of blood from the nick on his chin. "I even washed and combed my hair."

When they reached the front door, Zeke stood on the porch and looked off to the west at the gathering storm clouds, tinged crimson by the setting sun. He inhaled deeply and exhaled slowly as Willie led the way inside, cheerfully announcing, "We're here!"

The interior of the house was warm and bright. A fire jumped and crackled in the fireplace, and lamps and candles cast a flickering glow all about. The aromas of fresh baked bread and fried meat hung in the air, along with the scent of ground and brewed coffee. Nana was already seated at one end of the kitchen table, and Rebecca was just setting down a platter of venison steaks on it. She straightened up and wiped her hands on her apron. "Welcome, Zeke. I hope you're hungry," she said, smiling.

Zeke removed his hat and returned her smile. "Famished after today's work, Mrs. Stevens," he answered. "I'll wager Willie is, too."

He moved toward the chair at the side of the table nearest him, but she waved him away. "You can sit at the head of the table," she said. "It will be nice to have a man occupy that spot again. And I'd take it kindly if you would call me Rebecca."

"Happy to, ma'am . . . Miss Rebecca." Zeke went to where she'd told him. Rebecca sat down on the left side of the table, and Willie eased into the chair on the right. They all looked at Zeke expectantly, and it took him a silent minute to realize what they were waiting for. "I would say grace over this fine meal," Zeke finally said with a slight tremble in his voice, "but I don't have the words. Perhaps the other man at the table would do the honors?"

Willie's chest swelled with pride as his mother nodded her consent. She clasped her hands in front of her, bowing her head. Nana clasped her hands and bowed her head also. Zeke bowed his head, but his hands remained in his lap. "Bless us . . . oh Lord . . . ," Willie struggled to remember the words properly, ". . . for these gifts we are about to receive from your bounty . . . through Christ our Lord, Amen."

"Amen," Nana exclaimed. "Very good, Willie!"

As the platter of steaks, a bowl of common beans, and a plate of sliced bread were passed around the table, the wind picked up outside, and the windows rattled slightly in their frames. Zeke glanced upward. "I wish I had gotten to replacing those shingles on the roof before now," he said. "It will probably rain by morning."

"We should be fine," Rebecca answered. "We haven't had any leaks between the roof boards so far. I'll add a bundle of cedar shakes to my shopping list. If the weather clears by morning we can go into town tomorrow." Willie was happy to hear that news. He always enjoyed their trips into town because of the different sights to be experienced at Schneider's Mercantile.

"Good," Nana chimed in. "I can use some new spools of thread for my sewing."

"I'll be happy to go along," Zeke added. "Mule can use the exercise. The corral she shares with Molly isn't nearly big enough to suit her energy."

"It's settled then," Rebecca said. "We'll go in the morning if the weather is suitable."

After that exchange the remainder of the meal was consumed in near silence. Outside heavy raindrops could be heard plopping onto the roof and ground. The rain soon became a downpour as thunder rumbled in the distance above the sound of the rushing wind.

When Rebecca and Nana finished eating, they rose and began to clear the table. Zeke started to get up to help them, but Rebecca placed her hand gently on his shoulder as she passed, and he remained seated. Nana returned from the stove with two tin cups of steaming coffee, placing one in front of Zeke and returning to her seat with the other. When Willie's mother reclaimed her chair, Nana gave her a knowing look and then stared directly at Zeke as he sipped his coffee.

"So, Mr. Smith," Nana said with a chuckle in her voice. "How long are you going to keep up the charade?"

Zeke seemed taken aback by her question. He set his cup down on the table in front of him but didn't fully meet her gaze. "Charade?"

Nana sipped her coffee. "Let me tell you a little story about my journey out here many years ago. We were passing through New Mexico with a wagon train and stopped at an army post for a short rest and to resupply. I remember watching a ceremony on the parade ground. They awarded some sort of medal for bravery to a scout who had saved a patrol from the Apaches. The man's name escapes me right now, but that scout was a dead ringer for you. Much younger than you are now, of course, but your eyes and mannerisms are most unmistakable, even to my feeble old brain."

Zeke slumped in his chair. "How long?" he muttered.

"Have I known?" Nana replied. "Since the day you arrived a bit over a week ago and I first spoke to you at the gate. I figured you'd tell us who you really are when you thought the time was right. I just got tired of waiting."

Willie thought his neck would break from swiveling back and forth, following the conversation from one end of the table to the other. His mouth hung open in wonder at what he was hearing. Nana caught his glance and winked at him. His mother sipped her coffee and watched Willie's reaction as if without a care in the world. It was obvious the two women had spoken of this before tonight and had laid their trap carefully.

A flash of lightning illuminated the windows as Zeke sighed deeply and straightened up in his chair. "I was going to tell you," he began. "I really was, and I hope you believe that. My real name is Ezekiel Flagg, and I *was* that army scout you saw so many years ago in New Mexico."

To Willie's surprise, his mother and grandmother both reacted to that name when Zeke spoke it.

"I suppose I should tell you the story of

why I've been hiding from Ezekiel all this time," Zeke continued. "Before scouting for the army, I was a bounty hunter in Texas and Oklahoma. The work didn't pay all that well, but I was good at what I did. I could track like a Comanche, and my mind was sharp enough to put together little bits of information I heard and saw to find my prey once I was on his trail. If the criminal didn't want to go back with me to face justice, I would bring him back draped across a saddle. It didn't matter much to me which way they wanted it, and word got around that I was good with a gun. Pretty soon, men were looking me up to see who was faster and more accurate. They weren't, and I was.

"After a while those seeking to make a gunslinger's reputation by laying me low stopped facing me and started trying to shoot me from ambush instead. They failed, and I got tired of looking over my shoulder. I decided to hide out with the army in New Mexico. I signed up to scout against the Apaches. The campaigning was hard, and the fighting was fierce, but I learned all I could about my enemy and, armed with that knowledge, did my job without complaint.

"When I left the army, I drifted back into Texas and took a job as a marshal in a little border town called Rio Bonita. It was quiet there, and I only had to deal with an occasional drunk or scallywag. After my time in New Mexico, I thought I was finally forgotten about because nobody came looking to kill me. I was happy there . . . until a pack of horse thieves came to town."

CHAPTER 4

"Pain is relative to the severity of the wound. It can shape the course of our lives, or it can destroy us. But, thankfully, it can also prevent us from being too foolish."

Zeke paused to take a large gulp of coffee. Willie was suddenly aware of the total silence that surrounded them. The rain outside had stopped, and the wind had died down to a whisper.

"Please go on," Rebecca said. "What happened in Rio Bonita?"

"Wait," Nana said. She rose and went to the stove, picked up the coffee pot and a rag, and brought them back to the table. She refilled Zeke's cup, and her own when she returned to her chair, then set the pot down on the rag and leaned forward. "Let's hear the rest."

Willie watched Zeke pick up his cup and

cradle it in both hands as if he needed to warm them. A look of sadness came over his face as he stared into his coffee, and then he began to speak again.

"Well, there came a day — it must have been around this time of year — when a group of cowboys rode into town with a small herd of horses. I heard later they'd stolen them from somewhere in Mexico. They put them up at the livery corral and visited the local saloon to celebrate their ill-gotten gains. Sometime during their carousing they decided to rob the saloon and the general store to replenish their cash. They shot and wounded a clerk in the store and ran back to the livery to retrieve their herd and mounts. I came out of my office at the sound of gunfire just in time to see them stampeding their herd down the main street, shooting into buildings and whooping like wild savages as they rode by."

"Did you catch them?" Willie asked, wide eyed.

"I caught them, all right. But not before they killed somebody." Zeke shifted in his chair as if gathering himself. No one else made a sound. "Before I could snap off a shot at them, I saw a pregnant woman in the middle of the street, frozen in terror as the horses bore down on her. Those cowboys and stampeding herd trampled her down so fast I couldn't stop them." He paused and looked at them all, and Willie had the sense he was wrestling with something even more painful than what he'd already told them. Then, with a heavy sigh, he continued his story.

"I mounted my own horse and took off after them. I caught up with those thieves some ways out of town, and there was a sharp fight. When the shooting ended, I was seriously wounded, and they were all dead. I don't know how long I lay there bleeding my life out before two vaqueros happened upon the scene of carnage and discovered me. They patched me up as best they could and carried me with them to the hacienda of Don Enrique de la Rosa, where they worked, some miles away.

"They put me in a small *jacal* away from the main house and nursed me back to health with the help of Don Enrique's daughter, Manuela, and the local priest, Father Antonio. They were all Papists, and the priest gave me what they call the Last Rites so I could get into Heaven if I didn't survive. Heaven was a place I had never given much thought to getting into before, but I needed all the help I could get." A wistful smile crossed his face. "Manuela came to my bedside and read to me from her Bible as I lay unconscious and feverish for days. She changed my bandages, and when I finally woke up and was somewhat myself again, she fed me my meals. As I grew stronger, her company became more important to me day by day, and my feelings for her grew."

Zeke took another sip of coffee. "When I had recovered enough to get up and start moving around, we took long walks together. I asked her to explain her religion to me, having been on the receiving end of it for some time by then. I had never been overly religious, trusting more in my strength and wits to survive, so I was genuinely curious as to just how a strong belief in some higher power could affect someone's life. She gladly shared what her faith taught and meant to her. I was particularly struck by the idea of atoning for one's sins, or doing penance as she called it, because I felt I had plenty of those to make up for.

"I finally worked up the courage to tell Manuela how deeply I felt about her and asked her to come away with me. She turned me down flat. She admitted she cared for me but told me that she was already promised in marriage, as was their custom, to another man. He was the son of a successful merchant in Mexico City. She and her father would be leaving in a few days to meet her prospective husband."

"How hard that must have been," Willie's mother murmured.

Zeke nodded. "It was. At that moment I would much rather have been shot and wounded again. I decided then to start over. To end the life of Ezekiel Flagg and become a new person who would not make the same choices that resulted in pain and heartache. I determined that I would help people if I could and, by so doing, make up for all the harm I had done before."

His voice caught, and he tried to cover it with a feigned cough and a quick sip of coffee. Willie felt an unnatural shiver run up his spine as a sudden gust outside rattled the windowpanes. He imagined the wind as not so much heralding the return of the storm but as an unseen listener urging Zeke to go on telling the story of what had set his feet on the path he now followed. The boy rested his elbows on the table and cradled his chin in his hands, eager to hear more.

"So, what brought you here, then?" Nana asked.

Zeke rose from his chair and stretched. "Aren't you folks bored yet?"

"Not by a long shot!" Nana snapped. "You stop now, and I'll beat you with a broom. Sit down and finish your story!"

"Better do as you're told," Rebecca said. "Nana can be hell on wheels when she sets her mind to it."

"It *has* to be past Willie's bedtime," Zeke replied as he resumed his seat.

"I'm not tired at all," Willie responded.

Zeke smiled. "In that case, I'll keep going. In the days that followed, Manuela didn't come every day as she had done before. She did bring me a fancy suit of clothes to wear for the ceremony to be held at the de la Rosa estate when she and the wedding party returned from Mexico City. My old clothes were less than presentable, even though they were long since laundered and mended by the hacienda housekeeper.

"When the morning of departure arrived, my plans also were complete. The carriage Manuela and her father were to ride in and a wagon packed with trunks of clothing and supplies for the journey stood outside the front gate of the hacienda, along with mounted escorts, including the two vaqueros who had helped save my life. I walked up to them and wished them a safe journey. Just then, Manuela and Don Enrique came out of the gate. I shook Don Enrique's hand

and thanked him for his kindness in allowing me to recover from my wounds at his place. Manuela stood off to the side watching me, and I'm sure she could tell from my demeanor that I would not be there when she returned. After her father entered the carriage, she stepped up to me and hugged me close and kissed my cheek. Then I helped her up into the carriage. I still remember the sadness in her eyes as it pulled out of the yard and the caravan drove away.

"On my way back to my jacal I asked one of the stable hands to saddle my horse and bring it to the adobe hut. I neatly folded the fine suit of clothes Manuela had given me and placed them on my bed, donning the clothes I had arrived in. When the stable hand brought up my horse, I was surprised to see my buckled gun belt hanging from the saddle horn, my cleaned and polished badge pinned to the holster. My vaquero saviors had cleaned and oiled my pistol and rifle while I was recuperating, returning them to their proper places in the holster and saddle scabbard. I stuffed the badge in my saddlebags and buckled the gun belt on before mounting up.

"As I rode away, the stable hand called after me, 'Dios sea contigo,' which means

God be with you. I waved back to him, thinking to myself that I surely hoped so. I rode northwest from Ranchero de la Rosa and never once looked back. By sheer dumb luck, I soon approached the small local church that Father Antonio oversaw. He was standing out by a small corral watching his mule eating hay when I rode up. He welcomed me warmly as I dismounted, and I asked him if he would trade his mule for my horse. I thought it best to change mounts so there would be no chance of my being recognized riding Ezekiel Flagg's horse, and a mule seemed more fitting for the new life I planned to lead. He protested at first that the trade would be unfair to me but finally relented.

"I led my horse into the corral and unsaddled it, transferring the rig to the mule. As my horse took over chewing hay, I mounted up and rode the mule out through the corral gate and away from that little adobe church."

Zeke sighed deeply and sat back in his chair. "I named my new steed Mule, because I couldn't think of another name that seemed to fit her. Father Antonio was right when he told me she was a good mule. Even though she didn't understand a word of English at first, we learned about each other pretty quickly. She's been a good and even-tempered companion along the way out of Texas, through New Mexico Territory, and here to Arizona Territory. Occasionally, when I've found myself short of funds to keep us fed and taken care of, I've picked up odd jobs for whoever would hire me on. At various times I have been a store clerk, a freight wagon delivery driver, and a farmhand. I stayed away from law enforcement and ranching because I know they'll drag up painful memories. That's also why I never returned to Rio Bonita." He shrugged. "That's about it. I've been trying to help people wherever I found myself ever since."

A brief silence fell as they all absorbed Zeke's tale. Then Nana pulled the rag from under the coffee pot and blew her nose loudly into it. "Now you've gone and made me cry, you rascal!"

Willie's mother looked across the table at him. "Off to bed with you, young man. We've a busy day tomorrow."

Zeke rose from his chair and walked to the door. "Good night, all. I'll see you in the morning. If you still want me here."

"We do, of course!" Rebecca replied. "Good night, Zeke."

Nana, daubing at her eyes, just waved at him, and Willie, on the first rung of the lad-

39

der to the loft, called out to the closing door, "Good night, Zeke!"

CHAPTER 5

"A change of scenery every now and then is good for the soul."

The next morning was damp and misty, the remaining moisture on the roofs running down and plopping heavily into puddles on the ground below the eaves. Willie yawned as he pulled the canvas tarp from atop the woodpile, soaking his pants leg when water that had collected in the uneven recesses splashed him. He had fallen asleep almost instantly after crawling into bed the night before, but his dreams were troubled by visions of Zeke shooting and killing men. As he chopped wood for the stove, he wondered what could drive a man to commit such violent acts. But the thought of being afraid of Zeke never entered his head. There was an obvious kindness in the man that he greatly admired and appreciated. Besides that, his mother and Nana seemed quite taken with Zeke because he was a big help and a comfort to have around. He chopped the damp wood, his mind more on what Zeke had told them of his life than on the chore he was doing.

Nana walked by on her way from the chicken coop. "Stop daydreaming over that wood, Willie," she mock-scolded him. "I have to build up the fire and get the coffee started."

"Nana?" Willie looked up. "Something's been bothering me about what Zeke said last night."

She stopped and turned on the bottom porch step. "What is it, dear?"

Willie hesitated, embarrassed by his own curiosity about an adult subject. Still, he wanted to know. "Why do you suppose he left that Manuela lady so quickly? I would have stayed and tried to change her mind about marrying that other fellow."

Nana laughed and continued up the steps. "Ask him yourself, if you're so curious. He's right behind you."

Willie spun around. Zeke was, indeed, right behind him, standing with his arms folded across his chest and his head cocked to the side, a big grin on his face. He wore the same clothes as the night before but had buckled on his pistol belt today. His footsteps had been so silent on the wet ground Willie hadn't heard him approach.

"The reason's simple, Willie," Zeke began. "It's duty and honor. Manuela believed she had a duty to carry out her father's wishes. He wouldn't have picked a husband for her who couldn't provide for her comfort. I couldn't guarantee her that if she came away with me, and we both knew it. Rejecting her father's choice would have brought dishonor to the family name for breaking a contract both parties had agreed to. I left before she and I could grow any closer, believing it would be easier for her to forget about me if I wasn't around when she returned. I guess you could say I ran away so she could be happy."

Willie frowned, puzzling over it. Grown-ups were hard to understand sometimes. Zeke briefly laid a hand on his shoulder. "Come on. I need your help getting the wagon out from under the lean-to so you don't have to walk to town today."

They made their way to the far side of the barn. Willie knew exactly what his job was; he had helped his mother and Nana move and hitch the wagon before. He picked up the shafts, one in each hand, and backed up while Zeke pushed the small wagon out from under the three-sided lean-to. The wagon was more like a buggy, with one long seat in front that the two women sat on while Willie rode in the flat, open back used for hauling items. When the wagon was clear, Zeke said, "I'll get the tack and harness. You wipe any water from the seat so the ladies don't get their bottoms wet."

He tossed Willie his bandanna and walked around to the tack room at the rear of the barn. By the time he returned with the collar, harness, and reins, Willie had finished his chore and was wringing out the barely wet bandanna. Zeke tossed the gear into the back of the wagon, retrieved his damp neck scarf, and returned to the barn. He soon reappeared leading Molly. From inside the barn came the braying of its other occupant.

"Hush, Mule!" Zeke called out as he backed the horse up between the shafts. "You'll be next!"

In a matter of minutes, Zeke had Molly hitched up to the wagon, while Willie held her in place. Then they led the horse, wagon in tow, around the barn to the front of the house. Mule's racket from inside the barn continued without pause, and Zeke tossed the reins to Willie. "Tie up to the porch post while I go saddle that mule and bring her out. She'll be kicking the building down if I don't!"

Willie watched Zeke stride over to the barn and pull open the door. "You're making a liar out of me, Mule!" Zeke called out as he entered. "I told these people you were even tempered!"

"What's all that ruckus out there?" Nana's voice behind him startled Willie. He turned and saw her in the doorway, holding a steaming cup in her hand. "I thought I heard Zeke's voice out here. I've brought him his morning coffee."

"He's in the barn saddling Mule," Willie replied.

"Well, I'll leave it here on the porch for him. You come in for breakfast now."

She set the cup down on a small table beside the rocking chair she usually occupied in the evenings as the sun set. Casting one more glance at the barn, Willie answered, "Yes, ma'am" and followed her into the house.

He was on his second helping of eggs when there was a knock on the door, and Zeke called from outside, "All ready to go out here!"

"Would you like another cup of coffee?" Rebecca called back.

Zeke opened the door and poked his head inside. "No, thank you," he responded with a chuckle. "I don't want to have to stop too

45

many times along the way to water the bushes. Take your time. I'll just enjoy this beautiful morning."

A half hour later, after breakfast was done, and the dishes were cleared and washed, they were on their way to town. Zeke helped Rebecca and Nana up onto the wagon seat, handing the reins to Willie's mother, and swung Willie up into the bed. He walked Mule to the front gate and opened it and closed it after they drove the wagon through. Willie noticed that Mule practically pranced along behind the wagon, eyes and ears alert. She obviously enjoyed being out of the barn and corral and on the open, muddy road. The sky above was a pale morning blue, dotted with white cotton-boll clouds that hung there unmoving.

It only took twenty minutes before the Beecher place came in sight. Lean and lanky Tom Beecher was outside his log cabin building a stone wall. He waved at them as they passed, halting in mid-movement when he noticed Zeke riding with them. "Stop by on your way home," he called out. "The wife loves your visits!"

"We will!" Rebecca called back.

A little further down the road, Zeke rode up parallel to the wagon. "Seems like a nice enough neighbor. He the one that helps you out with fresh meat?"

"Sometimes vegetables, too," Nana answered. "He certainly helps keep our root cellar well stocked."

Rebecca nodded. "We might not have been able to stay on at our place if he hadn't."

The remainder of the ride into town was spent navigating the wagon around minor washouts where usually meandering streams had filled with rain in the higher country and turned into rushing torrents that washed over the road farther down. Once or twice Zeke had to dismount and push the wagon through deeper muddy spots too difficult for Molly to pull her load through unaided. Willie tried to jump out of the wagon bed to help push the first time they encountered such a quagmire, but Zeke had stopped him. "No sense you getting your boots muddy, too, young man," he said. "The sun should dry these spots out before our return trip. The drive home may be bumpier but faster."

Within an hour they topped a small rise, and the town of Pleasant Grove lay spread out before them. It stood on the intersection of two roads, the smaller one they were on and a larger one that cut diagonally across it. Four or five buildings lined both sides of the thoroughfares. Each road widened in town so a wagon entering from any of the four directions could easily turn around and head back out the way it had come in. People were walking along the wooden sidewalks, and the place was fairly bustling with activity.

"The mercantile first," Rebecca said as the wagon bumped down the gentle slope. "Then wherever else you need to go, Zeke."

Zeke touched two fingers to the brim of his hat. "Right you are, Miss Rebecca."

CHAPTER 6

"When trouble comes looking for you, the best thing to do is to meet it head-on. Hiding from it never makes it go away."

They pulled the wagon up in front of Schneider's Mercantile parallel to the wooden plank sidewalk. Zeke dismounted and tied Mule up to the hitching post, then took the reins from Rebecca and tied them there as well. As she turned in the seat to climb down from the wagon, he reached up and set his hands on her waist, lifting her and placing her gently on the sidewalk. "No sense in getting the hem of your dress all muddy. Slide over, Miss Nana." He repeated the process with the old woman, and she giggled like a schoolgirl. Finally, he turned his attention to Willie in the back. "You're on your own, Willie. Jump for it."

Willie leapt from the wagon bed to the sidewalk and followed the women through

49

the mercantile door. Zeke kicked the mud from his boots as best he could by banging the toes on the sidewalk and went in behind them.

Rotund Mr. Schneider greeted them warmly. "Welcome, Miss Rebecca, Miss Matilda, and young Master Willie!"

"Matilda?" Zeke asked with a laugh as he closed the door behind him.

"You hush up!" Nana snapped.

Mr. Schneider came out from behind the counter, wiping his hands on his apron. "Mr. Smith! Good to see you again. You are gainfully employed by this wonderful family now?"

"Thanks to you," Zeke replied as they shook hands.

The women had made a beeline for the bolts of fabric stacked neatly on shelves on the left side of the store while Willie stood in front of the candy counter nearby eyeing the multicolored confections on display. Rebecca stopped looking at fabrics long enough to walk over and hand Mr. Schneider the list of needed items she had written up for him. He studied the list and said, "I think I can fill this order for you, dear lady. In the meanwhile, the axe and shovel handles are in the barrel by the door. You'll find them fashioned of the finest hickory."

Rebecca turned to Zeke. "Pick out the handles that suit you." She returned to perusing the shelves of cloth, while Mr. Schneider vanished with the list into the storeroom.

Within minutes he returned, his arms laden with burlap and canvas sacks of supplies. He placed them on the counter as Zeke inspected the handles in the barrel, removing one or two to test their heft and inspect the wood for flaws. Nana had moved over to a display of sewing materials and had already picked out several spools of thread that were to her liking. Willie was now admiring a display of rifles and pistols hanging on pegs along the back wall. When Zeke had chosen the handles he wanted, he noticed several stacks of brown-colored hat blanks on a table near the front corner of the store. "Come over here, Willie," he called. "I think it's about time you had a proper hat to wear."

Mr. Schneider smiled. "Those are top quality hats. They came all the way from St. Louis, and some have the sweatbands already sewn in! The smaller sizes are on the bottom."

Noticing Rebecca's slight frown, Zeke said, "This is my treat, Miss Rebecca. I have a few dollars of my own, so this won't be

51

on your bill."

"Ah, yes!" Mr. Schneider exclaimed. "I almost forgot your bill! If you'll just step over here to sign it, Miss Rebecca."

While Rebecca waited at the counter for the storekeeper to finish writing out her items, Zeke and Willie were busy trying on hats. The smallest was too small, and the next size up was a bit large. "This might do," Zeke offered. "It has a sweatband in it already that can be stuffed with paper until you grow into it. We can steam and shape the crown and brim to your liking back at the house."

"It's perfect!" Willie announced proudly as the adults looked on.

Zeke approached Mr. Schneider at the counter as Rebecca signed her completed bill. "How much do I owe you?" he asked.

"A dollar should do the trick," the storekeeper replied. "Are you sure I can't interest you in a new hat, too?"

Zeke shook his head. "This hat has been with me so long it's almost a part of my scalp, even though it's seen better days. It could use some reshaping, so I'll do that when I do Willie's. I could use some oats for my mule, though."

Mr. Schneider nodded. "I moved the feed and grain two doors down from here to make room for more merchandise. My boy, Jacob, oversees that part of the operation and will be glad to help you there."

After saying their goodbyes to Mr. Schneider, the group carried their packages and sacks outside to load into the back of the wagon. Zeke helped Nana and Rebecca up onto the wagon seat, then untied Molly and handed the reins to Rebecca. "If you want to walk down to the feed and grain with me, you can tag along," he said to Willie, who had not yet climbed into the wagon bed with the supplies.

They started off together. As they passed the mercantile door, Zeke suddenly exclaimed, "The axe handle! I left it on the counter! You go on, Willie. I'll go get it and catch up to you."

Willie went on ahead down the sidewalk, watching his reflection in the mercantile window and admiring his new hat. Next thing he knew, he'd bumped square into someone. He looked up into the scowling face of Deputy Marshal Otto Manholtz.

"Watch where you're going, you little turd!" the brawny deputy bellowed and aimed a backhand slap at the boy. Willie ducked, but not fast enough. Big Otto's blow struck the top of his head, spinning his new hat off and knocking him to the sidewalk.

Before he could recover from the hit that had felled him, Zeke was suddenly there and kneeling beside him. Zeke laid the axe handle on the sidewalk, helped Willie back to his feet, and retrieved the boy's hat. The crown was dented in, and Zeke reached inside to push it back into shape before handing it to him. Then Zeke looked up at the hulking deputy standing there, legs spread and fists clenched.

"There was no call for that, mister!"

"What are you going to do about it, little man?" Otto growled in reply.

Zeke's right hand closed around the axe handle. He rose to his feet and swung it up between Otto's legs. There was a dull thump when the weapon struck home. Otto's mouth flew open, his eyes bulged out, and he bent over, grabbing at his crotch as a low moan escaped him.

"Just that," Zeke answered, bringing his arm across his chest and swinging the axe handle back and down to strike the side of Otto's head. "This, too!"

The big man fell off the sidewalk and landed face down with a splash in the muddy street. As a crowd began to gather, Zeke stood, looking down at Big Otto. The deputy rolled over and sat up, shaking his

54

head, sputtering, and spitting out brown water. Then, with a glare at Zeke, he grabbed for his half-submerged pistol in its holster on his right hip.

As Willie watched in awe, Zeke released the axe handle and pulled his own pistol. He'd cocked it and pointed it at Otto's face before the handle hit the sidewalk.

"Don't do that," Zeke warned. "You'll be dead!"

A voice behind Zeke spoke from the crowd. "An excellent suggestion, Otto. I would listen to the man."

Without taking his unblinking stare, or his pistol, off the man in the street, Zeke said, "Mister, if this fellow is a friend of yours, you had better step around where I can see you, or I'll blow a hole in his head big enough to ride a horse through!"

The man who stepped forward into Zeke's field of vision was well dressed and slightly taller than Zeke was. He sported a bushy white mustache, trimmed so as to not extend past the edges of his mouth. His eyes were small, narrow, and set close to his nose, and white hair peeked out from under his hat. Despite the white hair, his unlined face showed him to be a younger man.

"He's not my friend. He's my deputy. I'm Marshal Dave Seegern." He smiled insincerely as he tapped the badge pinned to the lapel of his frock coat.

"Am I under arrest?" Zeke asked, still not taking his eyes or aim off the big man sitting in the street.

"Oh, not at all!" the lawman exclaimed. "I witnessed the entire incident. You were perfectly within your rights to defend the boy and yourself!"

Chapter 7

"Whenever you succeed, if you can't be humble about it at least be quiet."

Marshal Seegern turned his head and called out to a husky man standing across the street. "Spinks! Get over here and help Otto back to the office and clean him up!" He turned back to Zeke. "Spinks is my other deputy. Otto will give you no more trouble — you have my word on that — so you can holster that iron. These people should disperse and go on their way now." The marshal glared at the crowd of onlookers as he spoke. Most of them avoided his gaze and began to nervously move away.

Rebecca, who had witnessed the entire incident from the wagon, climbed down from the seat, rushed to Willie's side, and hugged him. She scarcely glanced at Marshal Seegern, Zeke noticed. He watched as Spinks tiptoed across the street, as if trying to avoid stepping in the muddiest spots.

"Stop your pussyfooting, Spinks, and get over here!" the marshal shouted.

Otto had just staggered to his feet and begun wiping the mud off himself when Spinks reached him. The big man daubed gingerly at the bleeding cut on the side of his scalp, then draped his arm across the smaller deputy's shoulders. They turned and wobbled back across the street, Otto giving just one glance back over his shoulder at Zeke with pure hatred in his eyes. Only then did Zeke thumb the hammer of his pistol slowly back into place and return the weapon to its holster.

"You seem to have some experience with that," Seegern said with a nod toward Zeke's pistol. "If you're looking for work, I could use another deputy, Mister . . . ?"

"Smith," Zeke responded. "Thanks, but I already have a job."

Seegern gave another insincere smile. "No harm in asking. I should finish my rounds and go see how badly damaged Otto is." The marshal tipped his hat to Rebecca and strode away without another word. She watched him go with a stony expression on her face.

Zeke eyed her in silence for a second, then picked up the fallen axe handle and gave it

58

to Willie. "I better get down to the feed and grain to pick up those oats for Mule," he said. "If you think we can trust Miss Nana alone with the wagon, you can join Willie and me, Miss Rebecca. It shouldn't take long."

The three of them walked down to the feed and grain store. A small bell over the door rang merrily when they entered. Jacob Schneider was effortlessly hoisting a one-hundred-pound bag of feed onto his shoulder as they came in. He just as easily lowered it back down to the floor and tried to smooth his butter-colored hair when he saw them. "So good to see you again, Rebecca!"

Willie was amused to see his mother blush a little and straighten her bonnet. "Good to see you, too, Jacob." An awkward silence fell as the two of them stood smiling at each other.

Zeke stepped forward and offered his hand. "Name's Zeke Smith. I'm working out at the Stevens place. I need five pounds of oats for my mule."

"Of course!" Jacob replied. With effort, he looked away from Rebecca and walked to the counter, where he picked up a large metal scoop from beside a scale. He thrust the scoop into an open bag on the floor and emptied it into the bowl on the weighing device. He repeated the process and then read the weight indicated by the needle. "A little over five pounds be all right?"

"Fine," Zeke answered and dug for the money in his pocket.

Jacob bagged up the grain, and Zeke handed over the purchase price. As they walked back to the wagon, Zeke glanced at Rebecca, who was still smiling. "He's certainly a handsome devil, isn't he?"

"I think he's sweet on Ma," Willie chimed in.

"That's enough of that, you two," Rebecca snapped at them in mock anger. "Jacob is a very nice man!"

Nana scowled at them when they arrived at the wagon. She didn't speak as Zeke and Willie placed the bag of oats and the axe handle in the back with the other supplies. Still silent, she handed over the reins to Rebecca after Zeke helped her up onto the wagon seat, and Willie climbed into the back. Zeke untied Mule and swung up into the saddle. "Are we ready to go?"

"I've been ready to go since you street brawlers created such a scene!" Nana barked at him. "I can't believe you abandoned a helpless old woman and a wagon-load of goods like you did!"

Rebecca laughed. "If they were safe with anyone, it was with you, you she-bear." She coaxed Molly forward and turned her and the wagon back toward the road to their homestead.

As they headed out of town with Zeke riding along beside the wagon, several people on the sidewalks waved at them. "This is like a parade," Zeke remarked.

Nana laughed, though nervous strain lurked in her eyes. "You're the new local hero of Pleasant Grove. Big Otto's the town bully who has everybody terrified. His boss, Seegern, isn't much better. I never liked that man! That mustache of his reminds me of a white woolly bear caterpillar, and he has the eyes of a feral hog!" Her voice softened. "Thank you for coming to Willie's rescue. If you hadn't . . . well." She shook her head once, sharply. "Never mind that now. Nothing happened, and there's no sense borrowing trouble."

Zeke had been right about the condition of the road on the return trip. For the most part it was dry, although bumpy in places where the water had run over it and gouged out shallow furrows. Here and there a puddle remained that was easily avoided. It was in a lot better shape than the road in town, where the constant passage of wagon wheels, hooves, and feet had churned everything into a thick, muddy soup. The dried-up furrows left behind by the rushing water were not deep or wide, nor enough to stop the wagon wheels from easily passing over them. Zeke rode behind the wagon for the most part, where he could keep an eye on it. Only this time Willie saw him look back over his shoulder more often than he had on the drive into town.

In just under an hour they were pulling off the road at the Beecher homestead for the promised visit. "Hello the house!" Rebecca called out as she reined Molly to a stop in front of the Beecher cabin.

The front door flew open, and three children spilled out, all younger than Willie, followed by their mother and father. "Nana, Becca! Willie!" the children shouted gleefully but fell silent and retreated behind their mother's skirt when they spotted Zeke as he dismounted and tied Mule to the back of the wagon.

Tom Beecher called out a welcome as he moved forward to help Rebecca down from the wagon while Zeke helped Nana down on the other side. Willie jumped down from the wagon bed and joined the adults as

Rebecca introduced Zeke. "This is Zeke Smith. He's helping out at our place."

Beecher offered Zeke his hand. "I'm Tom Beecher, Mr. Smith. This is my wife, Mary, and I'll introduce you to all the children later."

"Call me Zeke. Mr. Smith is too formal," Zeke replied, tipping his hat to Mary.

Willie could not contain himself anymore. "Zeke beat the stuffing out of Big Otto in town!" he blurted out.

"Willie!" his mother scolded, but Tom laughed.

"Did he now? Well, I think that calls for a drink! I've got two jugs of hard cider I put up last year out in the shed, if Zeke would care to have a taste."

"I would be delighted to," Zeke replied.

Beecher turned to his wife. "Mary, why don't you and the other mother hens go inside for a cackle-fest while we roosters go imbibe? I think there's some regular cider out there for Willie. I know how the young ones pester him when he's here, and I think he would rather join us." He glanced at Willie and winked. "Isn't that so, young man?"

The women went inside the cabin, and Willie gratefully joined the men. As they walked to the shed, Tom chuckled. "So, you had a bit of trouble with Big Otto?"

"Nothing a stout piece of hickory couldn't resolve," Zeke answered.

The interior of the shed was cool and smelled of apples. Tom lit a lantern and pulled two earthen jugs down from a nearby shelf, handing one to Zeke. Several three-legged stools were stacked in the corner beside a workbench. He handed one each to Zeke and Willie, then took one for himself. He retrieved a third jug from a lower shelf, pulled out the cork stopper, and handed Willie the container. "This should be the regular cider, young man. You'll let me know if it isn't, I trust."

They settled onto their stools, and Tom grinned at Willie. "Now, tell me about Big Otto's downfall. I can hardly wait to hear the details."

CHAPTER 8

"Life sometimes seems like a series of mysteries we have to solve in order to move forward."

As Willie launched into the story, Zeke pulled the cork from his jug, sniffed the contents, and nodded his approval. He raised the jug to his lips, tipped it back, took a long drink, coughed once, and exhaled loudly through his mouth. "That certainly tickles your innards!" he said.

Willie kept on talking. When he finished relating his story, Tom whistled softly. "Oh, how I wish I had been there to see that altercation!" He shifted his gaze to Zeke. "How did the marshal take to your manhandling his enforcer like that?"

"He wasn't too pleased, even though he tried to hide it," Zeke replied. "He did offer me a job as a deputy, though. Is Pleasant Grove so rowdy that he needs three deputies to keep order? Seemed like a quiet enough place to me."

Tom shook his head. "Big Otto and Joe Spinks are there to carry out the edicts of the marshal, not to enforce the law. Seegern has his eye on a seat in the territorial legislature and has big plans for this community. He's the banker as well, so he owns the paper on just about all the businesses in town and the homesteads hereabouts. D'you know, he even set up the marshal's office and the jail in the same building as the bank? He likes to joke that it's the safest bank south of Flagstaff, 'because the law is always on the premises.' He acts like he controls everything already — him and his men."

Zeke leaned forward. "Give me a for-instance?"

"For instance, it's not unusual for the deputies to show up at a man's place and present a list of property improvements designed to enhance its value. They make it clear that those improvements must be done, or there will be dire consequences. Why do you think I'm building a stone wall out there where I didn't want one?" Tom took a long pull at his jug, then wiped his mouth with the back of his hand. "Nobody around here has the sand to stand up to his high-handed ways, certainly not me with a young family to think of. The only one who ever stood up to him was Will Stevens, and he's gone."

At the mention of his father, Willie felt a pang in the pit of his stomach.

There was a tapping at the shed door, and a tiny voice outside called out, "Papa? Mama says to come in the house. She made up ham and biscuits. Willie and Zee got to come in and eat."

"You tell her we'll be right there," Tom called back. He turned to Willie. "Run along with Francis, and take the cider jug with you. We'll be along directly."

After Willie had left the shed, Zeke asked, "How did Stevens die? I heard he was shot pursuing Apache raiders. Is that so?"

Tom looked taken aback at the bluntness of the question. "You sure don't beat around the bush, do you?"

"Shortest distance between here and there is straight at it," Zeke replied matter-of-factly.

"Well," Tom began, "it was about two years ago, as I recall. Somebody raided the Bidwell place, killed the Bidwells, stole their livestock, and burned the cabin and barn. Several of us saw the smoke and rode over to see what had happened, while Jack Hollis rode to town to get the marshal. Turned out Marshal Seegern was already on his way and met him on the road."

He took a fresh pull on the cider jug. "I got there first. Will Stevens, Stu Jenkins, and Pete Phillips arrived soon after. It was a horrible scene to behold. Hattie and Luke Bidwell were lying outside the house close to each other, shot full of arrows, and their cabin was ablaze. I found an Apache necklace on the ground near the bodies, so we figured Indians must have done it. When Hollis arrived with the marshal and the deputies, I showed everybody the necklace, and we took out after them. The trail of the stolen livestock was pretty easy to follow at that point, but we lost it in the woods nearby. The funny thing was, we started finding the stolen animals wandering around in the trees. Stevens, who was on friendly terms with the Tonto Apaches and knew them pretty well, kept saying it wasn't right for them to leave the livestock behind like that, even being pursued like they were.

"The marshal split us up into two groups to try and cut their trail in the woods. Stevens and Hollis went with Seegern and his deputies while the rest of us went another way. Pretty soon we heard two shots and then a volley of gunfire, so we raced back to the site where they'd come from, which was a small clearing in the trees.

"When we got there, Stevens and his horse were down, shot dead, the marshal kneeling beside them. The minute he saw us, he called out that the Apaches had ambushed them, and Big Otto and Spinks had charged after the raiders. We dismounted, ready for a fight, but right then the deputies emerged from the trees on the far side of the clearing, and Jack Hollis rode into sight a little bit away. He looked like he wanted to say something, but Spinks yelled out that the Apaches had run off, and there was no catching them now.

"We moved out into the middle of the clearing and discussed what to do next. Marshal Seegern insisted we go back, taking Will Stevens's body with us. Said he didn't want to lose anyone else to another ambush. So, we headed back to the Bidwell place, rounding up as many of the abandoned animals as we could along the way. We buried the Bidwells, then took Stevens home and buried him on the hill behind his house. It was a sad day." Tom's voice broke a little at the recollection.

Zeke took another long drink from his jug. "Seems mighty strange that the Apaches would shoot a man known to them and run away instead of gunning down the rest of you from hiding. Did Hollis ever say anything about it? Wasn't he with Stevens and the marshal's bunch?"

"Hollis didn't see what happened. Later on, when we talked about it without the marshal around, he said he rode into the woods to check out some movement Big Otto swore he'd seen deep in the trees. Time he got back, it was all over." Tom shrugged, looking grim. "Something stank about the whole business, but we didn't know anything for sure. All we could do was help the family to stay on by giving them supplies whenever we could and watching out for them. Since I live the closest, I was chosen to make deliveries and keep an eye on the place."

"I saw you," Zeke said quietly. "The day Willie and I fixed the front fence."

"You've got the eyes of an eagle," Tom said. "I thought I was pretty well hidden."

Zeke gave a half smile. "I'm an old hand at seeing people trying to hide from me." He paused, gathering his thoughts. "You think Marshal Seegern wanted Stevens dead?"

"I do." Tom braced himself on his stool, clearly feeling the effects of the hard cider he had consumed. "Lord help me, I do."

"Why?"

" 'Cause Stevens was the only one of us with the sand to stand up to him. Will Stevens kept a large amount of money in Seegern's bank, which would've gone belly up if he ever withdrew it all at once. There was also some talk around here of convincing him to run for the legislative seat Seegern wanted, though Stevens hadn't agreed to do it." Tom sighed, and his shoulders slumped. "He shouldn't have gone with the marshal on that posse, even with Hollis along. But he held the marshal and his deputies in such contempt as petty criminals, I don't think he believed they had the grit to actually harm him."

"Seems like they did," Zeke observed.

Tom stood up unsteadily and gave Zeke a crooked grin. "Say, would you like to see that Apache necklace? I kept it, you know. I hid it out here so the children wouldn't find it and be terrified."

"I surely would," Zeke said.

Tom staggered over to the workbench, pulled open a drawer, and rummaged around inside. "Not here," he muttered and pulled open another drawer. "Aha! Here it is!"

He withdrew an object wrapped in an old piece of cloth. He wobbled back to Zeke

71

and handed it over, then plopped heavily back down on his stool. "Ever seen anything like that before? Kind of pretty, isn't it?" he asked as Zeke unwrapped the necklace.

Zeke was deathly quiet for a minute, studying the artifact he held. Two pieces of leather were stitched together in the shape of a capital T, the crossbar four inches long and the upright twelve inches long, each intricately beaded by hand with geometric shapes. The rawhide thongs on the crossbar that held it around the neck had been cut, and the knot was still tied on the longer side. Blood on the beadwork and leather had dried black.

Zeke ran his finger slowly over the crusty residue. He couldn't keep the anger from his voice as he replied, "Yes, I have. It's very pretty, and it shouldn't have been there."

"That's just the way I found it," Tom fairly whispered, looking uneasy.

Zeke rewrapped the necklace in the cloth and handed it back. "Keep this safe and out of sight," he said. "There may be a day when I'll need to come and get it from you."

He stood up. "I think we better go join the others now. It would be best if nobody knows we spoke of any of this."

CHAPTER 9

"Life is like a placid body of water. It can appear serene on the surface but is filled with swirling currents underneath."

The inside of the Beecher cabin was alive with the shrieking of children at play and the voices of female conversation. They were warm, happy sounds that could always lighten any foul mood or heavy thoughts. As the men, cider jugs in hand, entered the room, Willie thought they both acted a bit tipsy, Tom more so than Zeke. He remembered seeing his father that way only once, laughing and happy after an evening in town spent at the Red Rocks Saloon drinking with a group of the other homesteaders. Willie's mother and Nana had acted upset with Pa at first when he arrived home drunk but had giggled at his slurred speech and efforts to remain sitting upright as he related stories and observations. Willie remembered feeling embarrassed that his father would befuddle his brain and act so foolish, but it *was* sort of funny.

After Tom and Zeke had seated themselves at the table, Mary set a plate of sliced ham and another of biscuits in front of them. As they began to eat, Willie eyed Zeke for signs of drunkenness. He secretly hoped Zeke was not the foolish sort and took comfort in observing that, so far, he did not appear to be.

Another hour was spent in pleasant conversation among the adults about the weather, the crop planting that was soon to begin, and other domestic subjects, while the children tired themselves out with their antics. Then Willie's mother announced that they had better be on their way in order to arrive home before dark. Everyone trooped outside to say their goodbyes. The Beecher children had warmed toward Zeke, still keeping their distance but no longer hiding from him as they did when he first arrived. Once the women were seated on the wagon and Willie was safely situated in the back, Zeke shook hands with Tom. "It's been a real pleasure," he said.

Tom clapped his hand on Zeke's shoulder and leaned in, murmuring something in his ear. Whatever he said made Zeke laugh.

Then Zeke mounted Mule, and Tom handed up the hard cider jug Zeke had been drinking from. "You may as well take this home and finish it, my friend," he said, grinning. "Bring it back any time, and I'll swap it out for a full one."

"I will do that," Zeke replied. He patted Mule on the neck and spoke to her. "All right, old girl, I hope you remember the way home, because I'm not in any shape to help guide you. If there's any doubt in your mind, just follow the wagon."

Zeke rode behind the wagon again during the drive home. Willie noticed him glancing back over his shoulder pretty often and staring intently at the sides of the road ahead. But he also whistled a few jaunty tunes softly to himself and cradled the cider jug carefully behind the saddle horn. Nobody engaged in much conversation during their time on the road, probably feeling all talked out, and Willie savored the silence after all the screaming of children he had just endured.

Molly's pace was quicker after her extended rest, Rebecca not easing her gait back with the reins, and they soon arrived home. As before, Zeke rode ahead to open and close the front gate for them. He remained at the gate after he shut it and stared down the road while Rebecca pulled the wagon up in front of the house, at which point he rode up alongside and dismounted to help the women get down and to unload the wagon.

"Where are we storing all these goods?" he asked.

"In the root cellar under the house," Nana replied. "The trapdoor is in front of the fireplace under the throw rug."

Zeke nodded, then wrestled a fifty-pound sack of potatoes out of the back of the wagon and tossed it up on his shoulder.

"Willie, you help take the smaller bags in. Once we're unloaded, we can unhitch, unsaddle, and rub down Molly and Mule. We'll feed them after we put the wagon away. Leave the axe and shovel handles in the back, along with Mule's oats, since they're going out to the barn anyway."

When he was smaller, Willie had been afraid to go down the steep steps into the root cellar. Although it was a large space, with stone walls and floor instead of dirt, the darkness always frightened him until the candle that sat on a rough-hewn table was lit. The flickering candlelight created dancing shadows among the shelves and tin-lined cabinets where supplies were stored that still made him uneasy. He shivered involuntarily, even though his mother and Zeke had gone down first, and all he had to do was proceed halfway down the steps to hand down the bags Nana gave him. Even the light streaming in from the open trap-door and his grandmother's reassuring footsteps on the wooden floor overhead did not comfort him in the cool semi-darkness, and he could not imagine how terrified he'd be at having to close and latch the door from the inside to hide from some disaster taking place above.

He was silently relieved when the storage task was complete and immediately went out to the front porch to calm his nerves. Zeke joined him there a few minutes later, and together they led the animals to the barn, where Willie held Molly while Zeke unsaddled Mule and turned her out into the corral. They unhitched Molly from the wagon next and turned her out also, then pushed the wagon backward under the lean-to. Zeke carried the harness and Mule's saddle into the tack room and brought out curry and dandy brushes while Willie carried the hickory handles and bundle of cedar shakes into the tool room. Then together they went out into the corral to brush the animals down.

■ ■ ■ ■

Chores at the barn done, Molly and Mule put up in their stalls for the night, Willie and Zeke walked back to the house. Rebecca and Nana were sitting on the front porch admiring the sunset. The sun rested on the western horizon, bright orange like a glowing fireplace ember.

"Are either of you hungry?" Nana asked from her rocking chair as they approached.

"Not me," Zeke replied.

"Me neither," Willie said.

"Well, hallelujah!" Nana exclaimed. "We needn't slave away over a hot stove tonight! What will we do with all our free time? How does a cup of coffee sound, Zeke?"

"I could sure use one," he answered as he sat on the edge of the porch by the steps.

Willie seated himself on the top step, and they all quietly watched the sun slip below the horizon. As the mantle of twilight settled over the land, Nana rose from her rocking chair and went inside to start a pot of coffee.

"This has certainly been an exciting day," Rebecca said. "I'm almost sorry to see it end."

Zeke shook his head slowly. "I'm glad

it's over."

Nana emerged from the house at that moment. "Glad what's over?" she asked.

"Glad today is over," Willie explained.

"Even though you became a folk hero?" Nana laughed as she sat down. "Zeke the Giant Killer has a certain ring to it."

"I took no pleasure in that," Zeke said softly.

Rebecca smiled. "Nor did Big Otto. Everybody else enjoyed it, though."

Zeke answered in a lighter tone, "My father always told me that if they're bigger than you, anything goes."

"He was a wise man, your father, and he raised you right," Nana observed. "Willie, go check on the coffee, and let me know if it's done."

When the boy had gone inside the house, she leaned forward and whispered to Zeke, "You made a powerful enemy today, my boy. I don't think his boss much cares for you either. I wouldn't go back into town for a long while."

"When I go back to town, I'll have a real good reason to," Zeke said ominously.

Willie emerged from the house just then. "I think it's done," he announced.

Nana rose and said to him, "Come help me bring some cups out."

79

They soon returned to the porch. Willie passed out tin cups to the adults, and Nana poured coffee from the pot she carried, its hot handle wrapped in a towel. As they sipped the steaming liquid, Rebecca said, "Since we women have a night off from cooking and washing dishes, why don't you two men take a day off from your chores tomorrow and maybe go fishing or something?"

"I was going to reshingle the roof tomorrow!" Zeke protested.

Nana waved his words aside. "You have something against doing that the day after tomorrow?"

Zeke sighed, then grinned. "Well, I've always found fishing a relaxing pursuit."

CHAPTER 10

"Every story has multiple parts that have to be fitted together in the correct order to be understood correctly and acted upon effectively."

The next morning, Willie awoke at the usual time. His mother and Nana were already up and about lighting the lamps in the kitchen, so he dressed, climbed down the ladder from the loft, and went outside to chop wood for the cook stove as was his habit every day. He was surprised to see a pile of kindling and small pieces of wood already stacked up on the porch just outside the door. After visiting the outhouse to relieve himself, he returned to the house, scooped up the wood, and went back inside.

Nana looked up from setting the table. "That was quick."

"It was already done and ready," Willie replied as he placed the wood on the floor near the cook stove.

"That man is a real gem," Rebecca said from where she stood over by the kitchen counter wiping out the dishwashing pan.

"One of us better marry him quick, before he gets away," Nana said with a chuckle. "I wonder if he prefers his women too old or too young?"

When Zeke arrived later for his morning coffee, Willie thanked him, as they sat together on the porch steps, for leaving the kindling for him to find.

"I had a sour stomach last night and couldn't sleep," Zeke said. "Strong drink tends to do that to me, so I took the axe and a log from the woodpile out to the barn, put an edge on the axe head with the whetstone in the tool room, and attached the new handle. Of course I had to try it out, and it works just fine. Just remember it's sharper now, so the next time you use it, be careful."

Rebecca came out of the house, wiping her hands on her apron. "Well, the breakfast dishes are done. I'm glad you two aren't on your way to the orchard pond. Nana is packing you a lunch right now."

"We only have one fishing pole!" Willie suddenly remembered.

"That's no big difficulty," Zeke told him. "You fish, and I'll just lie about and relax. It's been a long time since I've done that."

As Willie went inside to retrieve his fishing pole from his room, Nana came out onto the porch holding a burlap sack. "I put some pieces of meat gristle in here to use as bait," she told Zeke as she handed him the bag. "Don't eat them."

"No, ma'am," he answered.

Nana gave him a quizzical look. "Why are you wearing your pistol to go fishing?"

"Because," he replied, "I'm going some-place I've not been to before, and one never knows what to expect in a new place."

Willie returned with his fishing pole, no more than a straight stick with fishing line wrapped around it many times. The other end of the line had a hook tied to it.

Zeke held up the burlap sack and waggled it. "I've got lunch. Lead the way to the fish," he said with a laugh.

They headed off toward the pine woods a hundred or so feet behind the barn.

A slight breeze kicked up as Willie and Zeke entered the shelter of the trees. The sound of the air moving through the branches was like a welcoming sigh. In the travel way, wide enough for a wagon to pass through, was a small path worn on the forest floor that was nearly straight and easy to follow. Twenty feet in, they encountered the trunk of a fallen tree that lay directly across the path, roots like fingers clutching at the sky. Zeke broke off a few dead branches and tossed them aside, clearing an opening he could step over and Willie could climb after him without too much trouble. Once over the obstacle, Zeke stopped so suddenly that Willie nearly bumped into him from behind.

"What is it?" Willie said. "What's the matter?"

Zeke was staring at the dirt. "Somebody stood here behind this tree," he murmured, pointing at the ground to his left. He knelt down slowly and traced an outline with his index finger, not quite touching it. Willie could just barely make out what appeared to be the faint shape of boot prints side by side, toes pointing toward the downed tree, heel marks slightly deeper than the rest of the sole. A shiver ran down his spine.

"He must have come in from the direction we're going," Zeke said. "Stay to the right side of the path as we go on, and keep your eyes peeled for more tracks like these." Seeing the concern in Willie's eyes, he quickly added, "Don't worry too much; these aren't fresh tracks. The rain the other night nearly wiped them out."

He stood again and looked back across the tree trunk, down the path they had just walked. From this point he had a clear view of the back of the barn, the corral, and, offset to the right, most of the porch and the front door of the house.

Good sight line, he thought, be a long shot, but a decent marksman could make it. All he said was, "Let's go on and try to solve this mystery, shall we? Probably just a hunter who discovered he was on somebody's property and turned back."

They proceeded on down the path and made a game out of looking for other tracks. They did find a few more, going in both directions, and Willie seemed excited when he spotted one on his own.

In around ten minutes they reached a grassy clearing, a stream-fed pond in the center that was close to thirty feet across and fifty feet in length.

"The apple orchard starts on the other side of the pond," Willie said. "Nana and Pappa planted it themselves many years ago."

Zeke gazed toward the other side of the water, where the trees stood in even rows. Their branches were still bare of leaves, but clusters of buds were beginning to come out with the spring warmth. He looked around the clearing and observed a dry pile of horse dung just off the path to his right along with a few shod hoofprints. Willie, thankfully, had failed to notice either in his glee at reaching their destination. Someone had obviously tied up a horse to a nearby pine and walked in and out on the path. Zeke tried to remember if Beecher had mentioned riding over to check in on the Stevens place. He'd spotted Tom from a different direction across the road watching the front of the house and barn, not the back and side.

Willie's voice interrupted his thoughts. "My favorite fishing spot is on the orchard side. Follow me!"

They spent the rest of the day in quiet solitude in the grass beside the pond. Zeke did, indeed, find it a relaxing time. He lay on his back, hat over his face, enjoying the warmth of the sun and listening to the birds sing, but with his right arm across his body, hand resting on his pistol. Willie sat at the pond's edge, fishing line in the water, watching the breeze ripple the surface into intricate patterns of motion. When the sun was directly overhead, they unpacked and ate the lunch of fried egg sandwiches Nana had prepared. Willie propped his fishing rod on a Y-shaped stick pushed into the ground, then lay back on the grass and fell asleep.

He didn't know how long he slept, but Zeke's shout startled him awake. "Willie, you've got one! Wake up, and pull him in!"

He sat up. Zeke was at the water's edge holding the fishing pole, the line taut. Willie jumped up and rushed to Zeke's side, taking the pole just as Zeke's foot slipped off the bank and splashed into the water halfway up to his knee.

"Damn, that water's cold!" he exclaimed and quickly pulled his leg out. He hopped away a few feet and sat down heavily to pull his boot and sock off.

The sight of Zeke pouring water out of his boot sent Willie into fits of laughter. Zeke gave him a mock scowl. "Stop laughing at me, and land that fish!"

Between guffaws, Willie concentrated on the fish fighting at the end of the line.

CHAPTER 11

"The truth is a double-edged blade. In the right hands it can save you from harm, or it can cut you to pieces."

They arrived home in the late afternoon. From her rocker on the porch, Nana spotted them approaching and called out to Rebecca inside the house, "They're back! We can start supper now!"

Willie ran ahead, holding the burlap lunch sack they had carried out to the pond that morning. "I caught a big chub!" he shouted with pride. When he reached the porch he withdrew a foot-long, silvery-gray fish from the bag and showed off his prize.

Nana clapped her hands. "That's certainly a huge fish! Go inside and show it to your mother and then get washed up for supper."

As Willie rushed into the house, Zeke stopped in front of the porch. In a lowered voice he said, "Just so you know, we found boot tracks on the path that indicate somebody was out there watching the house. I don't mean to alarm you, but how many guns do you have?"

Nana stared in shock, then replied, "We keep a shotgun leaning against the wall just inside the door, but it's hardly ever loaded because there's a child around. The shells are nearby and handy, though. And Rebecca keeps William's old repeating rifle and pistol in her room."

"Anything else that could be used for protection?"

She thought a moment. "I keep my late husband's army saber under my bed, and, if I remember right, his old cavalry rifle is stored up in the hayloft out of Willie's reach. My Bryan was an officer in the big war back East. That man was quite a scrapper."

"It doesn't surprise me that he was. I'll have a look at that rifle," Zeke said.

"Are you expecting trouble?" she asked, a slight tremor in her voice.

He shook his head. "Not at present. But it's always better to be prepared. After Willie goes to bed, you, Miss Rebecca, and I should speak of this further."

At the supper table later while they ate, Willie regaled Rebecca and Nana with the story of his fishing trip. Zeke was relieved when the boy mentioned they had "found some tracks" only in passing. That indicated he was not as alarmed by them as he had seemed at first. His retelling of Zeke slipping into the water, and his hopping antics after, drew peals of laughter from the women.

"Still too cold for a swim, wasn't it?" Nana observed.

"It sure was," Zeke replied. "The inside of my boot is still soggy. I'll need to get some saddle soap or linseed oil on it before it stiffens up!"

Willie finished his story with how he had struggled to land the big fish.

"To the victor go the spoils," Rebecca said. "I'll gut and clean your hard-fought catch, and we can have it for breakfast tomorrow."

The meal finished, Nana began clearing the table while Rebecca heated water to wash the dishes. The house grew quiet except for the clanking of dishes as they were stacked up.

Zeke said to the women, "I'll help dry if you'll tell me afterwards how to prunc apple trees to get ready for this year's new growth."

Willie yawned deeply.

"Willie, you look all tuckered out," Rebecca said. "Why don't you slip off upstairs now?"

Eager for the warm comfort of his bed after a long day, Willie said his goodnights without protest and slowly climbed up to the loft. There was silence from above soon after, and Zeke guessed the boy had fallen asleep almost as soon as his head nestled onto the pillow.

The dishes done and put away, Zeke and the women took their coffee out onto the porch. Rebecca claimed the chair, and Nana settled into her rocker, while Zeke sat on the porch edge, dangling one leg off.

Once they were seated, Rebecca gave him a stern look. "All right now, what is all this secrecy about? Nana told me you wanted to speak with us after Willie went to bed."

Zeke sipped his coffee, took a deep breath, and then related what he had told Nana earlier about the footprints and the traces of a rider near the fishing pond. "Tell me about your banker marshal and his deputies," he said when the story was finished.

Nana pursed her lips. "I just knew that hog-eyed rascal was behind this somehow!"

"Hush," Rebecca scolded her, then spoke to Zeke. "Seegern was here when we arrived to join Will's parents, so I don't know much about him. I do know he managed to get himself elected town marshal under questionable circumstances, and he's won reelection ever since because nobody runs against him. I've heard rumors that Otto once killed a man with his bare hands, claimed self-defense, and did some time in prison for it. He showed up here shortly after Seegern was elected marshal, I'm told. Spinks was a local militiaman somewhere else in the territory and fought the Apaches before moving here around the same time as Otto. That's all I know."

Nana spoke up. "Mrs. Bacron runs the boardinghouse in town where Otto and Spinks rent rooms. She says Spinks decorated his room with Apache regalia he collected from dead warriors and villages that were attacked and captured. She also says he keeps a cedar chest full of scalps at the foot of his bed."

"Mostly from women and children, I'll wager," Zeke muttered.

"She says Otto gets drunk and breaks furniture, which he always pays for in cash when he sobers up," Nana added.

Zeke sipped his coffee. "Have you heard anything about the marshal sending his deputies out to the surrounding homesteads to force them to improve the worth of their property on his orders?"

Rebecca nodded slowly. "Mary Beecher mentioned that during our visit. Tom's building a stone wall, even though he says there's no point in it. The Bidwell place — what was left of it, anyway, after the raid two years ago — was practically leveled by workmen the marshal hired. The bank owns the land now and rents it out for farming." She frowned as if a fresh thought had struck her. "Jacob Schneider once told me, in confidence, that his father was pressured into renting an empty, bank-owned store just down from his place to run the feed and grain business out of when there was plenty of room for it in the mercantile. The Schneiders aren't the only merchants who've been bullied into things, either."

"Has anyone ever showed up out here making demands?" Zeke asked.

"No," Rebecca answered. "Seegern and his deputies all show up together once a year to deliver the tax bill. The money is withdrawn from my account at the bank after I authorize it, but the deputies have never come alone."

Zeke nodded. "That's good to hear."

"Well, you've aroused my curiosity now,"

Nana remarked. "Just what is this all about?"

"Maybe nothing, maybe everything." Zeke set down his coffee cup. "I'm sorry if this is painful, but Tom Beecher told me how Willie's father died. Maybe it's just the former lawman in me, but I'm suspicious about the details."

"I just knew the story they told us was wrong!" Nana snapped, then lowered her voice. "I always wondered why the Apaches used arrows on the Bidwells, but guns on the posse. Why not shoot more arrows, nice and quiet, and then slip away unseen? And how come my son was the only one hit? It never made sense they'd steal livestock and then abandon them, either, or burn the cabin down. Folks hereabouts came running the minute they saw the smoke."

Rebecca reached for Nana's hand. "Oh, my dear, why didn't you share your suspicions with me before?" she whispered.

Tears shone in the old woman's eyes. "Because I wanted so badly for our lives, yours and Willie's especially, to return to some sort of normal. I didn't want bad thoughts and what-ifs to tear our family apart!"

"Me either," Rebecca said, her voice small and quivering. She rose from her chair and stepped over to Nana, who stood up. They embraced, holding each other tight for a good minute. Zeke waited silently until they broke apart, returned to their seats, and composed themselves.

"So, what do we do now?" Rebecca's voice shaking, and in the lamplight filtering through the front window, Zeke saw tears on her cheeks.

"I'm sorry to have caused you this pain," he said. "For now, we don't do a thing. I'll gather more information on my own and let you know what I find."

"And Willie?" Rebecca asked softly. "He loved his father, and he's half grown now. He has a right to know."

"Better leave Willie out of this for the time being. I'll tell him when the time is right. You two act as normal as you can so as to not arouse any suspicion in him. It's hard enough for a boy to lose his father at such a young age, but knowing the truth of how it happened could be devastating to him, if it's not handled delicately."

"It won't be easy, but I'll try," Rebecca said.

"You already know I'm pretty good at keeping things hidden," Nana added. "But tell me one thing, Mr. Zeke Smith, why are you getting yourself involved in all this?"

The darkness hid his face as he replied, "For justice."

Chapter 12

"There is so much more to the world than just the small portion you can see around you. You have to keep moving to see it all."

The next morning, after the family had eaten breakfast, Willie had completed his lessons, and Zeke had finished his coffee, he went to the barn and carried the tall ladder stored there to the house.

As he leaned it up against the front porch and checked it for stability, he said to Willie, "Think you can handle a hammer well enough to help me put some new shingles on the roof today? It's a tricky process."

Willie said he thought he could handle the job, and they went to the barn to pick up the bundle of cedar shakes, a bag of nails, a chisel, and a hammer. On the way back to the house, Zeke stopped at the woodpile and selected a small piece of wood with as flat and straight sides as he could find.

Zeke climbed the ladder first, carrying the bundle of shakes, and from the porch roof he called down to Willie, "Toss that piece of wood to me and climb up."

Willie did so, then placed the tools in the bag of nails so he could carry them up more easily. He was halfway up the ladder when Nana stepped out onto the porch.

"Now don't you fall off the roof and break your leg, Willie," she admonished him with a chuckle. "If you do, we'll have to shoot you!"

"Aw, Nana!" he replied. "I'm not a baby!"

"I'll be careful, too, thank you!" Zeke shouted down to her. He reached out to take the bag of nails Willie carried, then helped him off the top of the ladder. Surveying the roof of the house, which sloped down to the porch roof they stood on, he said, "Be careful from here on. Try to step lightly on the side seams between the shingles. You don't want to break one by tromping on the middle of it because that'll just make more work for us. We can get started on that area over there where a few of the shingles are missing."

They walked carefully up to the site he had indicated. Zeke eased down to sit and used the chisel to pry up the front of the shingle above a bare spot so he could peek underneath it. "Good," he said. "It's not clogged with any wood from the missing shingle and the nails are clear of debris. We can drive a new shingle up there and onto the nails. The shingle is thinner at the top and the nails should rip through it without any splitting. The nail heads will hold it in place once it is underneath them. Then comes the tricky part." He demonstrated as he talked, putting a new shingle in place, holding the flat-sided piece of wood at the bottom of it and tapping it upward carefully with the hammer until the replacement shingle stuck out just a little longer than the bottoms of those on either side of it.

"Now I'll drive a skinny nail in at an angle here at the center, just at the lip of the shingle above. All shingles are thicker at the bottom because they're tapered that way." He plucked a nail from the bag and positioned it. "I'll use another, fatter nail to drive it in snug because I don't want to risk hitting the upper shingle with the hammer and splitting it."

Willie nodded, watching avidly. Zeke finished driving the center nail in, then placed the flat hunk of wood at the bottom of the new shingle again. "When I tap up until it's flush with the others in the row, the nail should bend as the wood pushes against it until the head flattens out and slips under the lip of the shingle above. Just like so!"

Willie looked amazed at the process, then dismayed. "I don't think I can do that."

"Give it a try," Zeke answered. "Not everybody is a handyman, but you won't know if you are or not unless you try."

Under Zeke's watchful eye and gentle direction, Willie nervously tried his hand on the next missing shingle they moved to and discovered that he could, indeed, do it. Even though he was hesitant and slow, he felt pride in his accomplishment and was grateful Zeke had encouraged him to make the attempt. Luckily, there weren't too many missing shingles, so Willie's lack of speed presented no real problem as they switched off, working on every other replacement. They finished the front side of the roof in just about an hour and then walked up to the roof peak to see what needed to be done on the other side.

"Just one spot over there," Zeke observed. "Why don't you enjoy the view from up here while I take care of the rest?"

"All right . . ." Willie gazed at the landscape stretching away below him, a wave of evergreen treetops interspersed with open areas where some trees were still leafless. He could make out the roads he had traveled on yesterday, snaking through the green blanket like light-brown ribbons. Rivers and streams sparkled in the sun as they flowed in and out of the shady cover. Flocks of birds swooped through the cloudless sky in an aerial dance that was fascinating to watch, above the greenery that seemed to undulate over hills and valleys all the way to the horizon, where stark, rust-colored mountains rose dramatically to enclose and protect the valley.

"Quite a sight, isn't it?" Zeke said from beside him. Engrossed in the view, Willie hadn't noticed that the sound of hammering had ceased.

"I can see the roof of the Beecher house with smoke coming out of the chimney!" Willie exclaimed. "I can see some roofs all the way in town from here, too!"

"Look over there," Zeke said quietly. "There's your fishing pond and the apple orchard."

"I've never seen the world from this high up before." Willie was smiling in wonder. "This is how a bird must see it."

Zeke nodded. "It's a sea of green, for sure."

Willie glanced up at him. "Have you ever seen the ocean, Zeke?"

"No, but I'm told it's like the biggest lake anyone could imagine. It stretches away for thousands of miles, and you need to sail across it in a boat just to see the other shore. They say there are prairies of grass east and north of here that are like an ocean, about as large."

"I want to see the ocean one day."

"When you're grown, I'm sure you will." Zeke smiled and patted the boy's shoulder. "But right now, our work up here is finished, so we better climb down before you sprout wings and fly away."

They walked to the edge of the porch roof, and Willie dropped the bag of nails and tools to the ground. Nana and Rebecca were sitting on the porch, Nana plucking a chicken and Rebecca sewing up a rip in the elbow of one of Willie's shirts. They looked startled at the metallic thud of the bag landing. Willie descended the ladder and waited for Zeke to climb down with the bundle of remaining shakes. When they were both on the ground, he asked Nana, "Chicken for supper?"

"No, Willie," she said with a grin. "I just thought this old hen would look better dead and naked, but I'll invite her to supper if you want!"

"We thought you might be tired of venison," Rebecca added.

"Boiled, baked, or fried chicken?" Zeke inquired.

"Hadn't decided yet," Nana said. "Do you have a preference?"

"Well," he answered, "I thought if you were going to boil it, we could use the steam to shape Willie's new hat. Whatever you serve will be fine with me. I'll eat just about anything that doesn't try to eat me first."

"Boiled it is, then," Nana announced. "I think there's some coffee left in the pot. I'll warm it up for you if you want."

Zeke smiled. "That would be most kind of you. Thank you."

"Do you plan to reshape your hat, too, while you're at it? I heard you tell Mr. Schneider that you might," Rebecca said.

Zeke touched the brim of his hat. "I suppose I could. Do you think it needs it?"

She laughed. "Not if you prefer looking like a vagrant hermit without roots anywhere."

Zeke laughed in return. "All this time, I thought I was!"

CHAPTER 13

"Days of innocence are gone all too soon. Savor them while you have them, because once they're lost to you, they become just fond memories, and you can never regain them."

Later, as they waited for the water in the pot on the cook stove to boil, Zeke explained the finer points of shaping a hat to Willie. Using his own hat as an example, he said, "I like to shape the crown with a small groove from the top down toward the front, halfway to the front brim, so water is channeled off. I put two pinch marks on either side of the crown in the front so I can remove the hat with my thumb and forefinger. You never take a hat off by grabbing the front of the brim. That weakens the fabric over time, and it droops to the point that no amount of reshaping can restore its strength. I curl the brim sides up a bit so they don't sag down and interfere with my hearing, and I turn the front brim down ever so slightly to keep the sun and wind out of my eyes, but not so much as to impair my vision. The backside of the brim I leave flat. With time, rough treatment, and exposure to the elements, your hat will start to lose its shape like mine has, and you'll have to redo it."

Willie looked at his own hat, turning it one way and then the other in his hands, as he tried to envision what it would look like if it were shaped like Zeke described. He decided he liked all the adjustments Zeke had talked about except the groove. He wanted the full, high, rounded crown because he thought it made him look taller.

Soon, the water in the pot was bubbling and jumping, and little billows of steam rose from the roiling, hot liquid. Zeke held his hat, brim down, in the rising cloud and moved it around to ensure every area was covered. Then he removed it from the rising steam, flipped it over, and began to push it with his fingers into the shape he wanted. For each area he worked on, he held it over the steam again long enough to soften it and make it more pliable. It took only minutes for him to be satisfied, and he placed the hat on his head.

"When it cools, it should retain its shape. Let me do yours now," he said to Willie.

"I don't want the groove in mine," Willie replied as he handed Zeke his hat.

"We want to look taller, do we?" Zeke winked at the boy as he held the hat over the steam. Willie blushed and wondered just how his friend knew that.

Nana poked her head in the doorway just as Zeke finished shaping Willie's hat. "Are you two going to use up all the boiling water? I have to pull that chicken out of there before it turns to mush!"

Zeke placed the still-warm hat on Willie's head. "Just finished, ma'am."

"If you boys aren't a couple of handsome devils!" Nana exclaimed as she stepped inside. "Rebecca! Come in here and have a gander at these two!"

As Zeke reached to remove his hat, Rebecca came in. "No, leave it on so I can have a look."

Zeke and Willie both smiled sheepishly as the women oohed and aahed at their hats with too much mock enthusiasm. "Now, Zeke, you finally look like you've put down some roots!" Rebecca announced.

"Speaking of roots," he said as he slipped his hat off, "while I was up on the roof, I noticed a patch of cleared ground to the west. Did you plant crops out there?"

"We tried a vegetable garden once," said Rebecca. "But it didn't seem to take."

"The critters ate anything that sprouted up!" Nana chimed in. "Not only that, the little critters hanging about attracted the bigger ones who wanted to eat *them.*"

"That always seems to happen," Zeke agreed.

"Wasn't worth the effort," Nana said. "Especially since the mercantile started selling local produce on consignment. We sell our extra apples there, in season." She moved over to the kitchen counter, picked up two cloths, and stepped over to the cook stove.

Zeke handed his hat to Willie and took the cloths from Nana. "Let me do that," he said and grabbed the pot handles. The fabric protected his hands from being burned by the hot metal. He lifted it off the stove and placed it in the empty wash pan on the counter.

As Nana began to prepare the evening meal, and Rebecca enlisted Willie to help her clean and sweep out the house, Zeke returned the ladder and roofing materials to the barn. While he was there, he climbed up to the hayloft and searched for the rifle Nana had told him was hidden there. He found it in a small alcove at the back end of the loft. It was wrapped and tied in a piece of denim, standing up out of sight behind two pine boxes in the darkened recess. He brought it out into the light, laid it on a bale of hay, and unwrapped it.

The weapon was a Spencer cavalry carbine from the Civil War era. With a twenty-inch barrel, it was shorter than the Winchester repeating rifle Zeke carried sheathed on his saddle but was a tough little weapon well-suited for a man on horseback to handle. Cocking the trigger guard lever ejected an expended cartridge from the top of the breech after firing while a spring tube in the stock, where seven rounds were loaded end to end, pushed a new round into the chamber. He marveled at the rifle's nearly pristine condition after so many years; someone had lovingly cleaned and oiled it for long-term storage.

"Where am I going to find cartridges for this antique?" Zeke mused aloud. Then the thought struck him to examine the pine boxes behind which the rifle had been hidden. When he moved the top box, its contents rattled. Prying off the top of the box with his pocketknife revealed it was half full of copper-cased cartridges and also held a cleaning kit. Although this rifle required that the hammer be pulled back manually after each time it was fired, cocked, and reloaded, it was still a powerful and useful firearm.

He rewrapped and replaced the rifle in its hiding place, then climbed down from the hayloft and walked back to the house. Rebecca and Willie were nearly finished sweeping dust and dirt off the porch.

"I was wondering if I could have the afternoon off, if you don't need me around for anything special," Zeke said to Rebecca. "I thought I might ride over to Tom Beecher's and return his empty cider jug. If you let Willie ride along with me, I promise to have him back in time for supper."

Willie looked at his mother with an imploring expression on his face. "Can I go, Ma?"

She smiled and leaned on her broom. "I suppose it will be all right. But take your coat. The wind's coming up from the north, and it will be chilly later."

As Willie ran into the house to get his garment, Zeke asked Rebecca, "Did Willie's pa ever teach him about handling a gun? I looked over the rifle Miss Nana told me about in the barn, and I think he should know it's there in case it's ever needed."

"He was too young before, but I'm sure Will planned to one day," Rebecca an-

109

swered, a wistful tone in her voice. "Do you think he wants to learn?"

"Every boy should be taught how to handle a gun safely," Zeke said. "I'll have a word with him and see if he's interested. If he is, I'll show him what he needs to know, if you're agreeable."

"It's probably time," she replied with a touch of sadness.

Willie returned with his coat just then.

"Let's go saddle Mule up and be on our way," Zeke said to him. "I hope you don't mind riding double. I think Molly should stay here in case she's needed."

They went to the barn, where Zeke buckled on his pistol, picked up his saddle and gear, and went out to the corral. Mule and Molly were standing there quietly, backsides to the rising wind, munching on a bale of hay. They greeted Zeke and Willie with a welcoming nicker and a bray as the two emerged from the barn. Mule stood placidly, more interested in eating hay, while Zeke saddled her up and wrestled her head away from her food in order to put her halter and bit in place. "Do you prefer to ride in the saddle, Willie, or to hang on behind?"

CHAPTER 14

"Sometimes everyday events you have always taken for granted can bring the most pleasure and comfort into your life."

As they rode toward the Beecher place, Willie in the saddle and Zeke behind it holding the reins and with his feet in the stirrups, the north wind increased in intensity. Willie clutched the empty cider jug in one arm and held onto the saddle horn with his other hand to keep from sliding sideways off his seat. With each wind gust he briefly let go of the saddle horn to press his hand on the top of his hat, even though he began slipping to the side each time he did so.

"Put the top of your brim down into the wind," Zeke advised him. "If the wind gets under it, your hat will blow away."

Willie tilted his head in the direction of the wind coming from his left. His hat stayed in place, allowing him to keep his grip on the saddle horn.

"Going back," he said without turning around, "I think I'll ride behind where you are."

Zeke chuckled at that. Fifty or so feet ahead of them three deer, a young buck and two does, broke from the cover of the trees and bounded across the road.

"There will be fawns out pretty soon, if there aren't some already hidden away in the woods," he mused. "Spring is my favorite time. Everything that grows is renewing itself, and new things are being born."

"I like it because it's warmer," Willie responded.

"Oh, there's that, too," said Zeke.

In the distance a rooster crowed, an unusual sound in the wild that let them know they were close to the Beecher place. Soon, they heard children's voices, and within minutes they were there. The stone wall Beecher had been working on earlier was higher and longer, but not by much.

"You've made some progress on that wall, Tom," Zeke called out as he spotted Tom Beecher staggering under the weight of a large rock he'd just removed from a pile on a sled hitched behind his horse.

Beecher turned around and set the stone down with a laugh. "I'll run out of ambition before I run out of rocks around here, that's for sure!"

Zeke dismounted and helped Willie down. As he shook hands with Tom, he said, "We brought your jug back."

Willie handed the jug to Beecher and walked over to join the children as they kicked a large pinecone back and forth in front of the cabin.

Beecher tucked the jug under his arm. "Do you want a refill?"

"For medicinal purposes only," Zeke replied. "Have you ever given any thought to selling this brew at the mercantile?"

"Come along to the shed," Beecher responded. As they walked, Mary Beecher poked her head out the front door, and Zeke tipped his hat to her. She waved in response.

They entered the shed, and Tom turned to Zeke. "You didn't ride all the way over here to discuss a business enterprise with me, did you?"

"Not really," Zeke admitted. "I was wondering if you could get all the men who showed up at the Bidwell place together so I can hear what they have to say about what happened to Will Stevens."

"You sound like a law dog on a scent," Tom observed.

"You could say that, but I'm just looking

for the truth to set things right," Zeke replied.

"Jack Hollis sold out to the bank under some pressure and moved over to the Prescott area shortly after the incident, but the others are still around, last I heard. I can get in touch with them and get them over here. Maybe we'll throw a neighborly get-together. Mary does love company."

"That would be just fine," Zeke said.

Beecher placed the empty jug on the workbench and grabbed a full one from the nearby storage shelf. "I better get some more of these out if there's going to be a gathering. Jenkins and Phillips are real thirsty boys," he joked as he handed the container to Zeke.

As they left the shed, a gust of wind nearly lifted Zeke's hat off his head, and he had to grab at it to keep it on. Over by the cabin, Willie stopped trying to kick the pinecone and giggled at the sight. Zeke grinned sheepishly.

"This wind should die down after sunset. It sure is a chilly one," Tom noted, eyes on the nearby trees swaying. He clutched his coat collar tighter around his throat.

"It will be nice to get back into the warm house at the Stevens place," Zeke agreed. "Boiled chicken for dinner tonight, and we have to be on our way. The ladies will skin me alive if I don't get Willie back home on time."

They said their goodbyes a few minutes later, the Beecher children pouting at losing Willie from their game. Out on the road, Zeke urged Mule into an easy trot. He sat in the saddle for the trip home, cradling the cider jug in the crook of his left arm, with Willie holding onto him from behind.

"Hang on tight," Zeke said over his shoulder. "I want to get us home as quick as possible; my hands are freezing!"

"Don't you have any gloves or mittens?" Willie asked. "I keep mine in my coat pockets."

"Hardly ever use them, especially on my right hand," Zeke replied. "A glove interferes with my finger sliding onto the trigger smoothly. You and I will have to do some shooting sometime, and I'll show you what I mean."

"Will you really teach me how to shoot?" Willie asked excitedly.

"I sure will," Zeke answered. "I've already gotten your mother's permission to."

"Really?"

"Really, and she's all for it. She even gave me leave to tell you about your grandfather's army rifle hidden in the barn."

"The one in the hayloft?" Willie responded. "I found that behind the boxes up there a long time ago."

Zeke laughed. "I should have known better than to think they had fooled you about that! I was a young, curious boy once myself."

They arrived home just as the north wind began to abate, like Tom Beecher had predicted it would. Zeke unsaddled Mule in her stall, rubbed her down, and gave her an extra portion of hay and oats while Willie went to the well to wash up for supper, then raced into the house to happily tell his mother and grandmother that Zeke was going to teach him how to shoot. The sun had just slipped below the horizon as Zeke placed his pistol belt on top of his saddle, put his jacket on, and strode out of the barn into the enveloping twilight. As he reached the house and mounted the porch steps, a shiver ran up his spine, and a prickly feeling settled in between his shoulder blades. He stopped momentarily in front of the door and glanced back over his shoulder, but nothing looked amiss in the silently gathering darkness.

"I must have caught a chill today," he muttered, then knocked on the door and opened it.

The inside of the house was bustling with activity. Nana was at the stove finishing preparations for supper while Rebecca and Willie were setting the table. A roaring fire crackled in the fireplace. The aroma of food and the warmth from the fireplace and cook stove combined to create a feeling of peace and contentment in Zeke, and he stood for a moment, hat in hand, basking in the sensation of home and family. He shook off a sudden, creeping sadness at what he had missed in life because of the path he had chosen. "What can I do to help?"

"Run out to the barn and fetch that jug you brought back from Beecher's," Nana responded. "I feel a chill coming on and could use a nip."

Zeke looked at Rebecca quizzically, and she nodded with a smile. "I think I could use one too."

Zeke ducked out and walked back to the barn, retrieved the jug, and returned to the house just as everyone was settling in to eat. He set the jug down on the table and took his own seat. Nana rose from her chair, grabbed the jug, and moved over to the cook stove. "I'll just heat some of this snake juice up in a pan; that should help warm our innards."

The boiled chicken and biscuits were tasty

and the company pleasant, even though Willie couldn't restrain himself from talking about being taught to shoot and how accurate he'd get with Zeke as his instructor. Amused at his boyish enthusiasm, the adults let him dominate the conversation, content to sip their heated hard cider and let the boy talk on.

"Maybe I can even go out and hunt for game," Willie said as he chewed on a piece of chicken.

"Don't talk with your mouth full, young man!" Rebecca admonished him.

Zeke smiled. "Guess I'll have to start the lessons with that rifle in the barn, then. The pistol can come later. It's always a good thing for the man of the house to know how to protect and provide for his family."

"Aren't you the man of the house now?" Willie asked.

"Oh, Willie." Zeke sighed wistfully. "I won't be here forever. That job will be, and is now, all yours."

Later, when everyone had finished eating, the table was cleared, and the dishes were washed, Nana dried her hands on her apron and remarked, "With Zeke around there aren't a lot of leftovers, are there? I've always enjoyed cooking for a man who eats hearty. I'll make us some coffee."

"It's easy to eat hearty when the cooking's so good," Zeke responded.

"A hungry man and a smooth talker to boot." Nana chuckled as she placed a handful of ground coffee from the Arbuckles' bag into the coffee pot and poured water in from a bucket kept on the kitchen counter. They sat around the table discussing the chores that still needed to be done around the place and when there would be time for Willie to begin his shooting lessons, while waiting for the coffee on the cook stove to boil. Willie was impatient to begin immediately and argued for sooner rather than later. Nana brought the tin cups of coffee to the table and passed them out, putting a pinch of sugar in hers from the sugar bowl. Zeke lifted his cup and took a small sip. As he started to set it back down, a sound caught his ear, and he stopped in mid-motion.

"Listen!" he whispered. "Horses!"

CHAPTER 15

"You can never know when unexpected events are likely to happen; you can only be ready to react to them to the best of your ability."

"I don't hear . . . ," Willie began.

Nana cut him off. "Shh! I hear them, too!"

"Out on the road," Zeke said tensely as he put his cup down and rose from his chair.

Willie heard the sound of galloping hoofbeats now, too. He ran to the door and threw it open and caught a brief glimpse of torches out by the front gate before Zeke grabbed his arm, threw him backward onto the floor, and slammed the door shut.

"Put out the lamps and get down!" Zeke shouted as a gunshot shattered the front window, spraying glass shards into the room.

As the women moved around on hands and knees, grabbing and blowing out the lamps, more shots rang out. Several bullets thudded into the door and the front of the house, and another windowpane exploded inward. The cabin was nearly dark now, except for the light from the fireplace. Whooping and shouting came from outside, although what the voices were yelling could not be clearly understood.

"My pistol is in the barn!" Zeke said, calmer now. "I need something to fight back with!"

"Wait!" Rebecca replied. She crawled toward her bedroom, returning a minute later with a pistol in one hand and dragging a rifle along the floor with the other.

"Give me the pistol," Zeke said. "You keep the rifle to cover me with. I'm going out there."

"Don't, Zeke!" Willie shouted from beneath the table.

Zeke's voice was flat when he answered. "This is what I'm good at, Willie!"

Rebecca slid the pistol across the floor. "The hammer is over an empty chamber," she told him.

Zeke waved Willie out from under the table and tipped it on its side, scattering chairs in all directions. "Thanks. Five bullets is all I should need if I can get to the barn," he said. "Come here, Willie, and close the door behind me quick after I go out. Miss Rebecca, when I open the door, you throw a rifle shot out there from behind the table, and I'll follow it. Miss Nana, see if you can load that shotgun and be ready for anybody trying to come in here, in case I don't make it."

Another volley of shots struck the house. Zeke and Willie stood up on either side of the door, as Nana sat on the floor beside it loading the shotgun. When she snapped the barrel shut, Zeke looked around the room at them. "Everybody ready?"

In answer, Rebecca cocked the rifle. He thumbed back the hammer on the pistol. "Now!" he shouted and threw open the door.

Rebecca fired the rifle through the doorway. Zeke dashed out and ran to his left along the porch. The rectangle of fireplace light streaming out from inside disappeared as Willie slammed the door behind him, but the brief illumination had given Zeke enough time to see the end of the porch and jump down to the ground.

More gunshots rang out, thudding into the house, as he lay on the dirt letting his eyes adjust to the darkness. At the front gate he could see four torches bobbing and weaving, as the men holding them struggled to control the horses they rode. The last flurry of shots that had followed his exit from the house had shown only three muzzle flashes coming from that direction. Zeke lay there for what seemed like an eternity but could only have been a matter of minutes, while his vision adjusted and vague shapes close by revealed themselves. As soon as he could discern the outline of the woodpile, he rose to his feet and moved over to it in a silent crouch. Kneeling behind the pile, he wished there were a full moon to give him more light to see by than just the stars twinkling overhead in the inky sky.

Angry voices drifted over to him, as if the raiders were arguing among themselves. Were the ambushers about to break off their attack and ride away? Zeke abandoned the idea of getting his own pistol from the barn and stood up from behind the woodpile. He took aim just below the torches and fired Rebecca's pistol three times. His last shot was followed by a shout of pain.

He knelt back down and fired a fourth shot over the wood, which was met by immediate return fire. He heard one bullet scream by him like an angry bee, and another smack into the woodpile, just as a numbing blow struck the right side of his head, and splinters showered his face. As he crumpled to the ground Zeke vaguely heard hoofbeats fading away into the distance.

His vision was clouded by thousands of pinpoints of light, racing back and forth and up and down like a swarm of fireflies. He felt warm blood flowing down the side of his head, cooling as it covered his cheek and dripped from his jaw onto his neck and chest. The only sound he was aware of was the noise of his own heart pounding in his ears. He struggled to his feet and staggered back toward the house, stopping and swaying like a drunken man every few steps until each wave of vertigo passed, and he could take a few more paces without falling down.

He reached the porch steps, grabbed a roof post, and eased himself up one foot after the other. He fell against the door, gave his customary knock with the barrel of the pistol, and shoved the bullet-scarred portal open. "It's me," he said, his voice weak.

By the flickering light of the fireplace behind them he could make out the dark silhouettes of Rebecca and Nana standing on the other side of the upturned table, rifle and shotgun pointing at him as he swayed in the doorway. Suddenly, the situation struck him as funny.

"Don't shoot me, ladies," he said. "I've already been shot."

Dark patches swirled at the edges of his

vision, and his slack fingers let the pistol slip from his grasp. It clattered to the floor as his knees buckled beneath him. Then everything was calming silence and comforting blackness.

CHAPTER 16

"When events begin to outpace you, you had better quicken your step to keep up, or you'll find yourself left behind."

Zeke drifted in and out of consciousness as Nana, Rebecca, and Willie dragged him out of the doorway and across the floor, then struggled to lift him into a chair. In his mind, the face of his lost love, Manuela de la Rosa, floated before him, as if returning to save his life again, a faint smile on her lips and a look of concern in her eyes. He reached out to touch her cheek tenderly, and reality flooded back in on him with a rush of sight and sound. He was touching Rebecca's cheek as she bent over him holding a lamp.

"Hold that light steady!" he heard Nana bark. "If I don't sew up this gash properly, he'll bleed to death right here! Willie! Wipe that blood away so I can see what

I'm doing!"

He felt a slight tugging at his scalp, and darkness engulfed him again. In his mind's eye he was locked in deadly hand-to-hand combat with an Apache warrior who kept hacking at him with a knife, cutting his chest, stomach, and arms as he tried to ward off the slashing blade. Once more, awareness flooded back over him, and he heard the ripping of cloth, then felt a splash of liquid that burned his wound and flowed down his face. Someone was wrapping his head in bandages, and Rebecca's voice floated around him as he fought to keep his eyes open.

"Willie, you hold the lamp and I'll try to pick the splinters out of his face."

"Will he be all right?" Willie's voice trembled on the edge of tears.

"I'm still here," Zeke croaked, his throat dry and raw.

"Well, stay with us and stay awake," Nana said from beside him as she wiped the side of his face clean with a damp cloth, being careful not to touch any of the splinters Rebecca was removing with her fingernails from around his left eye and forehead. "You took a nasty bump on the noggin out there, and if you fall asleep now, you may not wake up. I've seen that happen before."

"So have I," Zeke responded. His mind felt a little clearer now. "Any one of you hurt?"

"We're better off than you are." Nana patted his shoulder and went to the stove. "Well, they didn't hit the coffee pot, and it's not all boiled away. Want some?"

"I could sure use a cup right about now," Zeke said.

Rebecca pulled out one last splinter. "There! I think I got them all. If anything starts to fester, we'll know I overlooked one, and I'll go after it with a needle. Willie, give me a hand setting the table back upright."

Zeke started to get up to help them, but she forestalled him with a hand on his shoulder. "Don't you move from that chair, Mr. Zeke Smith!" she scolded him.

When the table was back in place, Nana set a cup of coffee down in front of Zeke. "So, what happened out there?" she asked as she turned a chair upright and sat down. Rebecca was moving around the room relighting some of the lamps they had extinguished just minutes before. Willie righted the rest of the overturned chairs and placed them back around the table.

"I got one of them," Zeke said as he drank his coffee. The hot liquid felt good on his dry throat. "I heard him yell out after I fired at the torches they carried. It was too dark to see them at all at that distance. I must have been grazed by a ricochet when I ducked down behind the woodpile, and they shot back at me. It sort of rattled my brain."

"Will they come back?" Willie asked quietly with a worried glance toward the broken glass littering the floor.

"Not tonight," Nana said. "They got a good taste of what will happen to them if they do. I hope."

A familiar voice called from outside, startling them. "Hello the house! It's Tom Beecher! Are you folks in trouble? Don't shoot me; it's Tom Beecher!"

Rebecca went to the front window and poked the muzzle of her rifle out through the missing windowpane.

"Come ahead, Tom," she called out. Then she turned to Nana. "You open the door when he gets here and keep your shotgun handy."

She kept a wary eye on the shadowy figure that emerged from the darkness and tied his horse to the porch post. He raised his hands as he mounted the porch steps and approached the door. "It's Tom Beecher," he repeated.

When Nana opened up to let him enter, Tom stared at the bullet damage in the door and at the broken glass on the floor as he stepped inside.

"What in the world happened here?" he asked breathlessly, lowering his hands. "I heard all the shooting. It sounded like it was coming from over here, so . . ." He moved toward the chair at the head of the table and sat heavily in it. "Lord, Zeke! Are you hurt bad?"

Zeke gripped the edge of the table, fighting a dizzy spell. "I'll be fine in the morning."

"In the morning, mister," Nana snapped, "we'll hitch up the wagon and take you into town to let Doc Carne have a look at you. He can decide if you're fine or not."

"I figured I better get over here to check on you all," Tom said. "After I heard the commotion, I came outside my cabin with a lit lantern just as some riders, three or four maybe, galloped by on the road. One of those bastards — excuse my language, ladies — actually took a potshot at me on his way past. So, I got my rifle, saddled my horse, and rode over here. On the way I saw three torches lying on the road, still burning, and another by your front gate, so I figured the trouble was here. What was it all about?"

"We have no idea," Rebecca replied.

"I plan to find out," Zeke said.

130

Beecher nodded. "I'll come back in the morning, help you get ready, and ride into town with you. I better get home now before Mary and the children make themselves sick with worry."

"Thank you, Tom," Rebecca answered. "Tell Mary we're all just fine over here."

"I will." Beecher rose from his chair, putting his hand on Zeke's shoulder. "You take care now, my friend, and get some rest. You're in good hands here."

After Beecher left, Rebecca got out the broom and began to sweep up broken glass. "We just cleaned in here," she muttered angrily.

"Leave that for tomorrow," Nana told her. "Nobody is going to wander around in the dark barefoot tonight." She glanced at Willie, who stood silently watching Zeke, every muscle tense as if he were trying hard not to cry. "We should all try to get some sleep now. We've a long day ahead of us tomorrow."

"I can make up a pallet on the floor by the fireplace for Zeke and throw an extra log on," Rebecca offered. "There's no way Zeke's sleeping in the barn tonight."

"Nor is he sleeping on the floor!" Nana snapped. "He'll sleep in my bed over there!"

"Just where were you thinking of sleeping, then?"

"I'll bunk with you, of course," Nana replied. "Your snoring won't keep me awake."

"*My* snoring?" Rebecca retorted, "*Your* snoring rattles the windows and dishware out here!"

Nana went to her bed and removed the quilt from it, then returned to Zeke. "Let's get that shirt off of you, it's ruined now anyway, those bloodstains will never wash out. I think I can salvage your jacket with a little work, though. You can wrap up in this, and we'll help you to the bed."

Zeke drew a breath to protest, but he knew well enough by now that she wouldn't change her mind, so there was no point in resisting. She began to unbutton his shirt while Rebecca wet a cloth to wipe off his chest once the shirt was removed. Zeke leaned forward while Nana moved around behind him and pulled his jacket and then his shirt off. Rebecca gasped when she saw the scars on Zeke's torso but said nothing as she washed the dried blood from his chest and draped the quilt over his shoulders. He rose unsteadily from the chair, and the women took hold of his arms, one on each side of him. Slowly and steadily, they

132

walked him over to Nana's bed. He sat down, then muttered, "My boots . . ."

"Don't worry about your boots," Nana said. "The bedding can be washed."

Exhausted, Zeke stretched out and rested his head on the pillow. Rebecca finished blowing out the lamps.

"Can I sit up with him for a while?" Willie asked.

"Of course. Throw an extra log on the fire, and get a blanket from Nana's cedar chest to wrap up in. Good night, Zeke." Rebecca moved toward her bedroom, and Nana followed.

"See you in the morning," Nana said over her shoulder and closed the door.

"Good night all," Zeke called after them.

In the silence, with the firelight casting a red, flickering glow over everything, Willie whispered, "Zeke?"

"Yes, Willie?"

"I was scared. Were you scared?"

"Every second," Zeke replied softly.

CHAPTER 17

"One day will follow another. No matter what today's circumstances are, there will always be a tomorrow to make changes in."

Willie awoke with a start the next morning, roused from his slumber by the sound of a pan clanking against another as his mother moved quietly about the kitchen. He was curled up in the chair where he'd dozed off last night, his legs tucked up under him, wrapped in a blanket, and facing the still-sleeping Zeke on Nana's bed. The fire had burned down to glowing embers. By that and the light of the few lamps that were lit, Willie watched the man intently until he could make out the rising and falling of his chest as he breathed. Satisfied that Zeke was indeed still alive, Willie rose from the chair, his knees stiff, and clutched the blanket closer around his neck.

"Do you need more wood for the stove?" he whispered to his mother as she turned from the counter with a stack of plates in her hands.

She shook her head. "No. There was plenty left over from yesterday. We'll need more for tomorrow, though." Gently, so as not to make noise, she set the plates on the table.

Nana silently entered the house with her basket of morning eggs. "That front door certainly has seen better days," she said, low voiced. "It's all shot up. So is the outside of the house around the windows."

"I'll make a list of how much board lumber and glass panes we'll need to make repairs. We can stop by the mercantile and place an order when we take Zeke to the doctor this morning," Rebecca replied as Nana set the basket on the counter.

"The eggs seem smaller this morning," Nana observed. "Those men must have disturbed the chickens last night."

"You think so?" Zeke rasped from the other side of the room.

"Well!" Nana answered, "Look who's back amongst the living!"

"Just barely," Zeke grunted as he sat up in the bed. "My head feels like somebody is beating an anvil in there." He swung his feet to the floor and stood on wobbly legs, draping the bed quilt around his shoulders. "Anybody seen my hat? I have to go."

"Just where do you think you're going, Zeke?" Nana snapped.

"To the outhouse, Miss Nana," he replied in an urgent tone. "I really have to go!"

Rebecca spoke to Willie. "Help Zeke to the outhouse, and take the kitchen slop bucket with you so you can empty it in there."

Zeke was already headed for the door. "I can make it to the outhouse on my own; it's not that far," he groused.

As Zeke left the house, Willie spotted the missing hat on the floor behind the ladder to the loft. He grabbed it and picked up the bucket of cooking and table scraps from the kitchen, then followed Zeke outside into the light of a brilliant yellowish-orange sunrise. He bounded down the porch steps and ran after Zeke, being careful not to spill anything from the bucket. Zeke was almost at the outhouse, which was situated just on the edge of a shallow ravine a short distance from the north side of the house. Willie slowed to a quick walk.

"I found your hat!" he called out.

Zeke ducked inside the small structure. The boy stopped where he was to allow his friend some privacy. About two minutes later, Zeke emerged from the outhouse, and Willie walked over to hand him his hat.

"Thank you," Zeke said. He tried to pull the hat on over the bandages encircling his head, but their bulk made it sit up too high. "Can you run out to the barn, feed the animals, get a clean shirt for me out of my carpetbag, and bring me my pistol belt? I better get back inside the house before Miss Nana comes looking for me with a switch."

"All right. Let me help you back, though, or Nana'll switch *me* instead."

They shared a grin, and Willie went to dump the slop bucket down the outhouse hole. When he returned, Zeke took the bucket from him, and they walked back to the house together in silence. He watched Zeke unsteadily mount the porch steps and go inside before he headed for the barn. Once there he tossed a few pats of hay into the stalls for Molly and Mule, checked their water buckets, then went into the stall where Zeke slept. He carefully removed the pistol belt from atop the saddle Zeke used as a pillow and located the carpetbag in the corner. The bag was made of heavy cloth, had two plain wooden handles on the top, and was held closed by a fabric strap sewn onto one side that fastened with a large wooden button on the other side.

Willie picked the bag up and carried it out of the stall, unbuttoned the strap, and opened it. Inside were several items of clothing: a pair of heavy canvas pants of the same brown color as the ones Zeke was already wearing, three pairs of wool socks, two undershirts, two pairs of drawers, a brown canvas vest, two bandannas, and two folded cotton shirts. One shirt was white with vertical blue stripes, the other bluish-grey with white stripes. Willie selected that one. As he pulled the shirt out of the bag, something fell from the folds of the garment onto the wooden floor with a metallic ping.

Willie picked it up. It was a bronze medal engraved with the word *Valor* and an image of crossed sabers beneath. The blue ribbon attached to it bore two vertical red stripes and looked faded with age.

Willie peered into the carpetbag. In the bottom of it was a partially open leather pouch, and Willie assumed the award had slipped out of it. He gently laid the medal back on top of the pouch, closed the bag, rebuttoned the strap, and placed it back in the corner of the stall. Then he wrapped the pistol belt in the shirt, settled both items in the crook of one arm, and left the barn.

Outside, Tom Beecher was just closing the

front gate and remounting his horse. He waved when he spotted the boy. "How is the patient this morning?" he called out.

"He's up and about but moving slowly, Mr. Beecher," Willie called back.

Beecher rode up and dismounted beside him. The horse nickered and curiously nuzzled the items the boy was holding. "Pretty exciting night last night, wasn't it?" Beecher remarked as they walked to the house together. Remembering his fear from the previous night, Willie just nodded.

When they went in, the table was set, and breakfast was put out, and Zeke sat at the head of the table sipping his coffee. Nana looked up from setting a bowl of scrambled eggs on the table. "Good morning, Tom. We set an extra place for you. Have you eaten already?"

Tom moved to the table and sat. "Yes, ma'am, I ate at home, but I'll have a cup of coffee if you don't mind."

Rebecca poured a cup and brought it to him. "We have sugar, if you want some for this," she said as she put it down.

"Just a pinch of sugar would be fine," Beecher said.

Willie laid the shirt and gun belt on the sideboard and took a seat. His mother and grandmother did also.

"Did you remember to wash up?" Rebecca asked Willie.

"I forgot. I was busy getting some things from the barn for Zeke."

She smiled. "So I see. I suppose we can let it pass this time."

While the family ate, Beecher asked Zeke what happened the previous night. As Zeke related the story, the women added a few details of their own. Willie ate silently, lost in his own memories of the events. In an unusually short time, the morning meal was finished. They cleared the table, leaving the dishes to be cleaned later so they could be on their way immediately to see the doctor.

"You stay here," Nana told Zeke sternly. "We don't need an injured man's help. Getting that clean shirt on is as much work as you're doing today, you hear?"

Willie went out with the others and fetched Molly, and Rebecca hitched the horse to the wagon. He went back inside, where Zeke had changed to the clean shirt and was buckling his gun belt in place.

"Looks like my jacket needs a wash yet," Zeke said, nodding toward the garment where it lay beside the wash pan on the counter. He wrapped the quilt around his shoulders again, then walked outside with Willie. The boy helped him climb into the

140

back of the wagon before joining him there, while the women took their usual seats, and Tom Beecher mounted his horse. From the barn, Mule brayed in protest at being left behind.

"She'll quiet down in a few minutes, after she realizes we're not coming back for her any time soon," Zeke told Willie as the wagon pulled out onto the road with Tom Beecher riding along beside.

CHAPTER 18

"Zeke was the best man to pick up on subtle clues I have ever met. It was almost as if he was a mind reader."

The ride into town was unexpectedly pleasant, the pale-blue morning sky filled with wispy clouds and the air warm, without a hint of a breeze. Tom Beecher kept up a constant chatter with Rebecca and Nana as they rode along, while Zeke and Willie sat silently in the back of the wagon enjoying the fine weather.

"We're thinking of inviting some families over to our place for a little get-together soon," Beecher said to the women as he gave Zeke a knowing look. "Sort of a celebration of the spring season ahead of us. Mary and I would be pleased if you folks would join us."

"That sounds delightful," Rebecca replied. "We could certainly use a bit of a respite from our routine."

Nana glanced over her shoulder at Zeke, still bundled up in her bed quilt. "When did having our house shot up and hauling wounded men around in the wagon become our routine?"

They all enjoyed a good laugh as the wagon topped the small hill overlooking the town and started down.

Doc Carne's office was two doors down from the bank on the same side of the street. Deputy Otto was sitting outside the bank on a chair, legs stretched and blocking the sidewalk, as Rebecca guided the wagon over. He stared at them intently as they passed him and pulled up in front of the doctor's office. Beecher dismounted, tied up his horse, and helped the women down from the wagon seat. Then he moved around to the back of the wagon, unlatched the tailgate, and helped Zeke slide down, leaving the quilt behind. As Willie climbed down to join them in the street, Otto called out, "Good morning, Mr. Smith." His voice dripped with malice as he continued. "You should really be more careful wandering around in the dark out there, you know, you're liable to hurt yourself!"

"Oh, I'll be more careful, Deputy, you can rest assured of that," Zeke called back as he

143

stepped up onto the sidewalk with the others.

They walked in silence to the doctor's door. "He's a real nasty one, that Otto," Tom whispered to him as they entered the office behind Rebecca, Nana, and Willie. "How could you be so pleasant to him?"

"Because he just told me everything I needed to know."

Tom's eyebrows rose. "He did?"

"Sure." Zeke grinned. "How did he know I was outside in the dark when I got hurt? For all he *should* have known, I could have just fallen off the roof this morning."

The front room was empty, but Doc Carne emerged from a side door, wiping his hands on a cloth. He was a tall man, his hair as white as fresh snow, with wire-rimmed glasses perched on the end of his nose.

"Well," he said with a chuckle, "this is the busiest morning I've had in a long time! I just finished treating a gunshot wound in the next room, and now here's a head wound!"

"Gunshot wound?" Zeke asked.

"Yes. Says his pistol went off while he was cleaning it last night. It's a shoulder wound, went straight through, and, given the slight upward angle, I'm not so sure of his story."

144

"Excuse me, I want to have a word with your patient." Zeke stepped past Doc Carne, then turned at the doorway of the examining room. "You and Tom should come, too. I may need witnesses."

All three men entered the room. A shirtless man, right arm in a sling, sat on one end of the examination table struggling to put on his shirt with his good arm. Tom closed the door and laid a reassuring hand on Doc's shoulder as Zeke stood in front of the man, hands across his body at belt-buckle level, the fingers of his right hand drumming on the handle of his pistol.

"The name's Smith, Zeke Smith," he said quietly. "I'm going to ask you a question, and if you lie to me, you're a dead man."

The fellow went pale, and his gaze darted around the room as if searching for an ally or a quick way out. "Ask away, mister," he stammered.

"How did you really get shot?"

The man hesitated, then heaved a deep sigh of resignation. "I won't lie to you. I didn't shoot myself by accident. My name is Del Forbes. Me and my partner, Bob Sullivan, brought a load of freight from Prescott in our wagon yesterday. It was almost dark by the time we finished unloading so we decided to have a few drinks in the saloon before bedding down and heading back to the Prescott freight depot today.

"We met the town deputies in there, and we all drank together for a while. They kept complaining about this fella who made them look foolish in front of their boss, the marshal. They said the marshal told them that if they weren't happy about the situation, they should do something about it. So they were going out to this fella's place to let him know he wasn't welcome and chase him off. They asked if we wanted to go along and have some fun treeing this fella, and we agreed. We rode out there with torches and started whooping and hollering, but then the deputies started shooting at the house." Del shook his head. "Bob joined in — he's always been a hell-raiser, but I drew the line at that sort of fun right there. Before I knew it, somebody was shooting back, and I got hit. So we left. Was that you fired at me, mister?"

"It was," Zeke replied. "Did you know there were women and a child in that house?"

"Oh, God, no!" Del exclaimed. "Was anybody hurt?"

"Thankfully, no," Tom Beecher said before Zeke could.

"Are you going to press charges?" Del

146

asked. "I'm real sorry, mister, really I am."

"No point if the marshal set this all up," Zeke answered. "He'll protect his deputies, make sure you and your partner shoulder all the blame. That's why the deputies asked you along in the first place." He folded his arms across his chest. "I have some advice for you, though. When you get back to Prescott, you request a different delivery route, and don't come back here any time soon."

"You have my word that I will, mister, and thank you!" Del sounded close to tears.

Zeke's hard expression softened. "Kind of funny that the only man who wasn't shooting at me winds up being the one I shoot. Let me help you with that shirt, and not a word of this conversation to your partner or the deputies before you leave town."

Zeke draped the right side of Del's shirt over the man's shoulder and fastened the top button so it wouldn't slip off. "I'll see you to the door," Tom offered as he picked up a hat from a nearby chair and handed it to Del. "Doc, you and Zeke might as well conduct your business since you're already in the examination room."

"Tell the ladies and the boy they can come in if they wish," Doc said as Tom and Del left. He gestured Zeke toward the table.

"Have a seat, Mr. Smith, and let's have a look."

When Tom returned, everyone was standing in the examination room, and Doc Carne had just finished removing the bandages from Zeke's head.

"My, my, this sewing is excellent!" the doctor exclaimed. "Who did this?"

"I did," Nana answered proudly.

"Couldn't have done better myself." Doc smiled at her. "But I would have used a different color thread. White is so ordinary."

Before Nana could form a sarcastic rejoinder, he continued, "I'm joking, dear lady. If you ever need a job, I can use a good nurse, and a midwife when birthing season rolls around soon."

"I already have a job keeping these three in line," she replied.

"So I see." Doc went to the medicine cabinet and brought out a roll of gauze bandage and a bottle of antiseptic. "Now remember, these stitches have to be removed in ten days, or they'll fester. If you don't want to make the trip all the way back here, I'm sure our lovely seamstress can do the job quite ably."

Willie was almost certain he saw Nana blush a little at that remark.

Doc poured some liquid from the bottle

onto a cloth and daubed it on the wound. He cleaned all the scratches and small punctures on Zeke's face, removed a few tiny splinters Rebecca had overlooked, and picked up the roll of gauze. "I'll just rewrap this, and we'll be done."

"Don't use too much of that," Zeke said. "I want to be able to put my hat on and have it fit."

"Not to worry, young man. One turn around your head should do the trick," Doc assured him as he worked.

He finished the job a short while later, and they walked back into the front room.

"If you write out an invoice for your services, Doctor, the bank will pay it on my signature," Rebecca said.

The doctor nodded. "Fair enough. I do have one question for you folks, though. What did you use for antiseptic on this wound?"

Rebecca looked sheepish. "Hard cider, I'm sorry to say."

Doc gave a hearty laugh. "I thought he smelled like apples!"

CHAPTER 19

"Make a plan and stick to it, no matter what obstacles you may encounter."

They left the doctor's office and stepped out onto the sidewalk. Otto was gone from the chair in front of the bank. Off to their right, the freight wagon, Del Forbes's partner Bob at the reins, was just heading out of town. Zeke and Tom stayed with the wagon as the others walked across the street to the mercantile in search of panes of glass and cut lumber to repair the house with.

"That was an interesting turn of events in there," Tom said to Zeke as they stood in the street at the back end of the wagon. "What are your plans now?"

"Get together with the other posse members and get their stories, for starters," Zeke answered. "Judging from what Forbes told us about the actions of the marshal and his deputies, I'm beginning to believe several murders were done here by one, or all, of them."

Tom's eyes widened. He glanced around to see if anybody was within earshot, but the street was nearly empty. "Will Stevens, you mean?"

"Him, yes. Maybe also the young couple who died in that so-called Apache raid."

Tom gave a low whistle. "So what can we do about it?"

"Once we get all the details together, we send word to the county sheriff so he can come here and handle it."

"What if he won't do anything? Seegern has a long reach; he knows and controls a lot of people."

Zeke looked grave. "We handle it ourselves if we have to and face any consequences after."

Tom shook his head. "That's a tall order. But I'd rather be on your side of it than opposing you."

"Thanks, Tom," Zeke replied. He glanced up. "Here comes Miss Rebecca."

Rebecca crossed the street, her face lit with a big smile. "They have everything we need in the stockroom," she told them. "I'll move the wagon across the street so we can load it up."

The two men followed the wagon as

Rebecca drove it over and stopped in front of the mercantile. When they all went inside to pick up her purchases, Mr. Schneider made a big fuss over Zeke's injury, apparently believing he had gotten it falling off the roof, and also complimented him on the job he had done shaping Willie's hat. They loaded the lumber in the back of the wagon, leaving the tailgate down because the boards were longer than the wagon bed. Zeke wrapped the panes of glass in the quilt he had worn earlier, separated from the tin of glazing putty, so they wouldn't crack or break if jostled on the way home. The whole while, townspeople passing by whispered among themselves, and many stared openly at Zeke and Tom as they worked.

"You seem to be somewhat of a curiosity hereabouts," Tom finally said as they finished loading the wagon. "You're the man who stood up to Big Otto and won!"

"Maybe it's not such a good idea for you to be seen with me, then," Zeke replied.

"Are you fooling? I'm proud to be seen with you! Besides, Otto saw us together when we pulled in. He probably added me to his enemies list then and there!"

Zeke snorted, then sobered. "All the same, keep your eyes peeled from now on."

After everybody climbed aboard the

loaded wagon, Tom went back across the street and mounted his horse, and they left town. When the wagon topped the rise, Nana turned in her seat and eyed Zeke. "Now that we're out of range of prying busybodies, what went on in the doctor's office? That pale-looking fellow with his arm in a sling kept apologizing to us on his way out."

"I shot him last night," Zeke replied, never taking his eyes off the road behind them. "He was with the bunch that raided your place."

Willie frowned, looking puzzled. "Then why isn't he in jail right now? Why didn't you have him arrested?"

"Because he wasn't alone. He and his partner were duped into being there. The marshal put his deputies up to it so there'd be someone to take the blame. Justice won't be served by corrupt lawmen."

"We're going to have to get the county sheriff involved," Tom added as he rode beside the wagon. "We have to put an end to Seegern and his boys' shenanigans and their riding roughshod over the people around here."

"Well, I say it's about time!" Nana exclaimed. "We need a good uprising around these parts, and we need it soon!"

"What we need right now is to get the house repaired," Rebecca said. "The uprising can wait."

They rode along in silence for some time after that, and Willie fell asleep leaning against Zeke as they sat in the back of the wagon. The restless night he had spent, the rhythmic creaking of wheels turning, the warm sunshine, and the steady clip-clop of the horse's hooves lulled him into a deep slumber. Zeke slid his arm around the boy's shoulders and smiled contentedly, despite his misgivings about the situation unfolding before them all.

Willie awoke with a start when the motion of the wagon stopped. They were at the front gate, and he had slept all the way home.

Tom dismounted and opened the gate for them. "I'll help unload and then be on my way. I have to go further on down the road and extend a few neighborly invitations to my get-together," he said as they drove past him through the gate.

"Drive up to the front porch," Zeke told Rebecca. "We'll unload the lumber there so it will be at hand for me to work with tomorrow."

"Will you be in good enough shape that

soon to do such a heavy chore? We can help."

"Believe me, Miss Rebecca, if I need help I will certainly welcome it. One good night's sleep without a headache like last night and I'll be just fine. In the meantime, I think I can get those windowpanes puttied in before dark to keep the heat in the house tonight."

She reined Molly to a stop in front of the house. Zeke, Willie, and Tom unloaded the lumber and glass onto the porch. A raucous braying arose in the barn when Mule heard their voices, and Zeke finally walked over there to calm her down and turn her out into the corral. Once the wagon was unloaded, Tom and Willie drove it around to the lean-to, unhitched Molly, turned her out in the corral, and put the wagon away while Zeke went in the house to begin replacing the shot-out windowpanes. Nana began sweeping up the broken glass on the floor while Rebecca climbed down into the root cellar to get some meat and potatoes for dinner.

When Tom and Willie came into the house, Nana said to the boy, "You're not finished yet, young man. I need some wood chopped for the stove if you want to eat tonight." Willie went back outside to the woodpile and set to work with the axe, happy to be back at his normal routine.

"I'll be taking my leave now," Tom said. "I've got some riding yet to do, and you've put me in mind to get home as quick as I can for my own supper."

Zeke stopped what he was doing and extended his hand to Tom. "Thanks for everything you've done, my friend."

"It was my great pleasure to be of some help." Tom grinned as he clasped Zeke's palm. "I hope to be useful again when you need me."

He stepped out and closed the door behind him. Zeke went back to removing the broken pieces of glass and putty that remained in the window frame. Suddenly, Tom's face appeared in the opening Zeke was working on. "Aren't you glad they weren't better shots? You would be replacing every pane instead of just one or two!"

He was still laughing heartily as he mounted his horse, waved to Willie, and rode to the front gate. Soon after Tom left, Willie came into the house with an armload of chopped wood. Zeke had just finished puttying the new panes in place on the inside and asked the boy to hold the panes steady while he went outside and applied putty to the exteriors. Looking through the window, Willie giggled a little when he noticed that Zeke stuck the tip of his tongue out of the corner of his mouth as he concentrated intently on his work.

CHAPTER 20

"Some things you learn in your life are right, and some things you learn are wrong. But everything you learn helps make you a complete person. Never stop learning."

That evening during their meal, as they discussed the next day's repairs, Willie noticed that not as many lamps were lit around the inside of the house. He made no mention of that fact because he knew it gave his mother and grandmother some comfort, and secretly he felt the same way. The warm light from the fireplace was enough for him to feel more at ease and less of a target, but he wondered just how long the semi-darkness in the house at night would last. Nana mentioned that she had made a thorough inspection of the inside walls and had found only three bullet holes, two above the fireplace and one in Rebecca's bedroom door, plus a nick in the ladder to the loft. She had also found a spent bullet on the kitchen floor and had swept it up along with all the broken glass.

"It could have been a lot worse had they been sober," Zeke remarked. "I'm just glad they didn't try to ride in and fire the place with their torches."

"If they had, you would have shot them all dead!" Willie blurted out.

"I certainly would have tried to," Zeke said matter-of-factly.

"What's done is done," Nana said with a heavy sigh. "Now we have to fix the damage and get on with our lives. Like we've always done."

"Starting with cleaning a whole day's worth of dirty dishes from this morning and tonight," Rebecca observed.

"I'll dry, if Willie will help me," Zeke offered, and Willie agreed.

"As a reward, in the morning I'll heat up a tub of water and try to wash the bloodstains out of your coat," Nana said to Zeke. "But I fear they have set in by now."

"As long as it's still wearable, I'll be happy," Zeke replied.

She chuckled in return. "I like having you around, Zeke; you're so easy to please."

■ ■ ■ ■

Later, after the dishes were done and dried, there was a small argument over coffee about Zeke wanting to sleep out in the barn that night, with the women being against it. He prevailed by insisting that Mule and Molly missed his company. As the hour grew late, Willie finally climbed up the ladder to his loft bedroom at his mother's prompting, and Zeke called after him, "Good night, Willie. Thanks for watching over me last night. If I can make good progress tomorrow with the repairs, I think we can start your shooting lessons in the afternoon." That exciting thought kept Willie awake, listening to the dying fire crackling and popping in the fireplace, for a long time after everybody else had gone to bed.

The next morning dawned unseasonably warm, the sky covered with low-hanging clouds that had drifted in overnight and, like a blanket, had kept most of the previous day's heat from escaping the land's surface. Overhead, a flock of geese flew over from south to north, unseen in the clouds, their passing marked by their raucous honking. Willie was already hard at work at the woodpile. Even though he had done his chore the previous day for the cook stove, more wood would be needed for Nana to heat water in order to wash Zeke's coat and any other laundry. The boy stopped for a moment to listen to the geese calls fade away into the cloudy distance. Zeke's approach from the barn, bag of nails and a hammer in hand, interrupted Willie's listening, as did Rebecca's calling from the front door that breakfast was almost ready.

"Let me help with that," Zeke said as he bent over to gather up the chopped wood. "You go wash up, and I'll see you inside."

Willie went to the well, drew a bucket of water from its depths, and placed the bucket on the stone edge. The liquid was cold and bracing, and he sputtered when he splashed it on his face from cupped hands and then rubbed his hands together in the bucket afterward. He untied the bucket from its drop rope and carried the nearly full container back to the front porch for Nana to heat and use later with the tub, washboard, and bar of lye soap she always used to scrub clothes.

When Willie went into the house, Zeke was already seated drinking his morning coffee and Rebecca was just placing fried eggs from the skillet on the plates around

161

the table.

"We used to have a bucket of whitewash out in the barn," she was saying. "I don't know how much is left, or what condition it's in, though."

"I saw it in the tool room when I was looking for a pry bar," Zeke responded. "I'll have a look at it later, after the boards are replaced. I'll start outside with the door and walls so as not to disturb Willie's morning lessons too much. The inside can be done later."

Breakfast over with, Willie fetched a large metal pan and started hauling water in from the bucket on the porch. Nana heated it on the cook stove, and from there Willie hauled the hot pan back out to the washtub Nana had set up. The heated water gave off clouds of steam in the cool morning air when he poured it into the tub. Once enough water had been removed from the bucket, Willie brought it inside and placed it next to the stove so the heating process would go faster without so many trips in and out of the house. When Nana was satisfied there was enough hot water in the washtub, she dropped Zeke's coat in to soak, along with her bed quilt and her pillowcase he had bled on. She stirred them occasionally with a stick while waiting for the water to cool enough to put her hands in and begin scrubbing.

Meanwhile, Zeke had gone back to the barn to feed the livestock. When he returned, he was whittling a point on the stub of a pencil. Willie noticed he was wearing his pistol again, a habit he had gotten out of before the recent trouble.

As the morning lessons progressed, Willie found it hard to concentrate on his studies with all the strange, new noises coming from outside the house. The screech of old nails being removed, the crackle of aged wood, and the sound of new boards being sawn intruded on his thoughts. The sharp *thwack* of the boards being hammered into place caused the dishes at the sink to rattle slightly, while the sound of Nana scrubbing and splashing in the washtub while she and Zeke talked was oddly comforting to him amid the changes being made outside.

Presently, Zeke opened the front door and let it swing back and forth a few times. He'd nailed four new boards in place of the bullet-riddled ones.

"The balance seems right, and the latch still works," he said. "The slugs don't appear to have gone all the way through to the inside boards; the wood was too strong and

163

thick to allow that. This place was solidly built."

Rebecca's smile was tinged with a pang of regret. "My husband insisted on that. We talked a few times about adding another bedroom to the house and expanding our family, but it never happened."

"May we use the old door boards for target practice?" Zeke asked gently after a moment. "They'll be useful when I teach Willie to shoot."

"Please, Ma," Willie said, when she didn't answer right away.

Rebecca blinked, as if she'd briefly been lost in thought. "Of course," she said and went back to her housework.

In the early afternoon, after Nana had hung the wash on the line to dry and Willie had completed his lessons, Rebecca brought Zeke a cup of coffee out on the porch. "I'm sorry about my wool-gathering earlier," she said. "I was a little lost in memory, I guess."

He accepted the coffee, and the apology, graciously. "No harm done, Miss Rebecca. Happens to me all the time, and I have a lot of memories to rummage through."

She sighed. "Memories can be trouble-some, can't they?"

"Not all of them, I suppose," he replied. "But many are. That's why it's important to keep making as many good ones as you can." He sipped his coffee and looked out over the yard. "I think it's time to give Willie his shooting lessons now, so he will have some good memories to carry forward with him."

CHAPTER 21

"Never shoot someone who doesn't deserve it."

Shortly after Willie had wolfed down a quick lunch of bread and fried bacon, Zeke went to the barn and returned with the rifle from the loft. He carried the weapon, still wrapped in its denim covering, in the crook of one arm and, in his other hand, his hat with a handful of shells in it. Willie carried the old door boards as they walked out to the front fence. The sun peeked from behind puffy white clouds overhead, and a gentle breeze rustled over the landscape as they set the boards against the fence posts, and Zeke used the stub of the pencil he had measured and cut with that morning to scrawl circular targets on the wood.

"Can you see those?" he asked Willie as he unwrapped the rifle. When Willie nodded, he continued, "We'll back off about twenty-five paces to start, and if you do well, we'll increase the distance from there."

When they had walked off the proper distance, Zeke showed Willie how to load the rifle. That done, he cocked the weapon and handed it to Willie, explaining to him how to line up the sights on the target. "Take a breath and hold it when the alignment's comfortable, then gently squeeze the trigger."

Willie's hands trembled a little when he took the rifle, held it up to his shoulder, and sighted in on the first board target.

The sound of the rifle going off wasn't as loud as Willie expected, but was still louder than he had prepared for, and his eyes shut involuntarily. The recoil against his shoulder wasn't what he expected either, more like a poke than an impact, and he wondered if that was because his wood-chopping chores had strengthened his arms and shoulders.

"Did I hit it?" he asked breathlessly.

"Dead center!" Zeke exclaimed. "You're a natural! Now tip the barrel up slightly and cock the lever. That will help gravity eject the expended brass. Point the barrel down a bit when you pull the lever back and chamber a new round."

Willie did as Zeke told him. Behind them, from the front porch, he could hear faint applause from Nana and his mother as they stood and watched. He glanced over and waved to them, smiling broadly, as Zeke said, "All right, you're reloaded, so hit the same spot again."

For the better part of an hour, they reloaded the rifle and fired at the four boards. After each series of shots they moved further away from the targets, with Zeke offering pointers on how to adjust sighting for the new distance and any wind that kicked up. Each time Willie aimed the weapon, he felt more at ease and confident in his newly acquired marksmanship.

Suddenly, Zeke placed his hand on Willie's shoulder. "Hold up there," he said quietly. "I hear a wagon coming up the road. Always be careful not to put anyone in danger by mistake."

Willie pointed the rifle at the ground and listened. Within moments, the boy could hear the jingle of harness, the creak of turning wheels, and the steady clip-clop of horse's hooves on the rocky ground as a wagon approached from the east. Zeke walked to the gate and peered over it down the road, then unlatched it and swung it open, calling out over his shoulder to the house, "It's the Beecher clan come to visit!"

As the wagon drove past him, Zeke waved

to the occupants and closed the gate, then walked back to Willie. He took the rifle and unloaded it, then rewrapped it in the piece of denim, stuffing the unused shells into his pants pocket.

"Put this away in the barn for now," he said. "I'll show you how to clean it later, after all the children have left. Scoot now, before they get too curious about what we're up to."

The wagon had reached the house when Zeke walked up beside it. Nana and Rebecca stepped down from the porch to greet everyone. Tom was admonishing the children in the back as Zeke arrived, "Nobody get out, we can't stay that long!"

He jumped down from the driver's seat, handing the reins to his wife, shook Zeke's hand and tipped his hat to the women. "Ladies and gentleman, you are hereby invited to a little neighborly shindig at the Beecher place next Sunday, if you're available. We're on our way to town to pick up a few essentials and wanted to see if you needed anything." He slung his arm around Zeke's shoulders. "Let's walk a bit, friend Zeke; we have some things to discuss."

They walked toward the barn. Tom reached into his coat pocket and withdrew an item wrapped in a familiar piece of cloth.

"I thought you might want to keep this necklace," he murmured. "My place is going to be full of prying young eyes in a week, and I might not get the chance to give it to you without someone seeing me."

Zeke took it and slipped it into his pants pocket atop the unused rifle shells.

"I also thought to invite Mr. Schneider, his wife, and their son, Jacob, to our gathering," Tom went on. "They've had some trouble with the marshal and his crew in town, most everybody there has, and Schneider is a man of letters. I thought he might write the message to the county sheriff about what's going on around here. It might carry more weight if a smart businessman is included in the complaint instead of just a bunch of dirt farmers."

"That's a good idea," Zeke agreed.

"Have you ever met Mrs. Schneider?" Tom continued with a grin. "She's not in the mercantile much, but she bakes delicacies at home to sell in the store. Don't tell Mary I said this, but that lady makes the best pastries in the territory. They sell out fast when you can find them there."

Willie came out of the barn just as the two men reached it. Tom smiled at the boy. "Putting your popgun away so my brood wouldn't pester you about it?"

"Yes, sir," Willie replied.

"How did the target practice go? From the spacing of the shots, I figured that was what was going on. It didn't sound like a gunfight, so I didn't hurry along, and then I saw the targets you set up. I've had some experience with all that; I did a stint in the army back East. Marching and target practice was about all we did when they could spare the ammunition, which wasn't too often." Tom laughed as they started back toward the house. "Half the boys in my outfit couldn't hit the broad side of a barn standing inside it. That's why when my enlistment was up, I sought gainful employment elsewhere as a civilian. The very thought of possibly going into any kind of a battle with that bunch just terrified me."

They reached the wagon, and the children peppered Willie with questions about the shooting they had heard and the rifle they had seen him holding when they arrived. Before climbing up to his seat on the wagon, Tom shook hands with Zeke and Willie both, giving Willie's hand an extra squeeze. "You listen well to what Zeke teaches you, young man. I have a strong sense that he knows exactly what he's talking about."

Willie smiled broadly. "Yes, sir, I sure will,

and I know he does."

Tom took the reins and turned the wagon to head back out the gate.

"Willie, follow them out and open and close the gate for them," Rebecca said. As Willie jumped down from the porch and ran after the wagon, she turned to Zeke. "So, how well does he shoot?"

"He's steady and a good marksman," Zeke answered proudly. "Maybe later on I'll let him try his hand with a pistol."

"You can use my husband's pistol, if you wish," she responded. "I think Willie will like that. You're a good teacher, Zeke Smith, and I'm happy you came here."

"We all are," Nana chimed in. "This old place sure livened up when you arrived."

As they watched Willie running back toward the house after closing the gate behind the Beecher wagon, Zeke waved him off to the side. "Get the rifle and cleaning kit from the barn first!" he called. "After we clean it up, we'll try your hand with a pistol!"

Willie let out a whoop and turned sharply toward the barn without breaking stride. He disappeared inside while the adults stood on the porch and laughed at his unbridled glee.

CHAPTER 22

"The one person you know best, and can always count on, is yourself."

Zeke and Willie sat on the front porch while Zeke supervised the operation of cleaning the rifle, allowing the boy to do most of the work. He told Willie how to disassemble it, remove the carbon deposits with brushes, oil the working surfaces, put it back together, and rewrap it securely. Rebecca came out of the house as they finished, holding the pistol she kept in her room and a box of cartridges.

"Here, Son," she said, holding the pistol by the barrel and handing it to Willie grips first, then offering the box of ammunition to Zeke. "It needs to be reloaded from the other night. I've been just too busy to remember to do it."

"Papa's pistol?" Willie said quietly as he hefted the weapon, testing the weight and feel of it. The connection with his father almost overwhelmed him, and tears welled up in his eyes.

Zeke said, "Well, we best get out there and get started before we lose the light."

Nana was out at the clothesline inspecting Zeke's coat. Despite her hard scrubbing, not all the bloodstains had come out of the inside of the collar.

"Zeke," she called out as they walked by toward the front fence, "have you ever wanted a black coat? I can dye this black, and it should look just fine."

"It looks just fine to me now!" he called back with a chuckle, then leaned over and whispered to Willie, "Let's see how long that sticks in her craw before I let her dye the stains over."

Willie was still giggling when they paced off the distance to the target at the fence. Zeke loaded the pistol, then handed it to him in the same way his mother had.

"I did a five-chamber load," he said. "The hammer is over an empty chamber. It's a safety idea so if the hammer gets knocked, the firing pin won't strike the cartridge primer and fire. I've never seen it happen in a holstered pistol, but it's better to be safe at this point. Later on, you can decide what you're comfortable with and how you want to carry it, with five or all six chambers loaded." Willie kept the barrel pointed down as Zeke continued. "The hammer pulls a little hard, so use two hands on the grips and both thumbs to cock it if you need to. For now, use the sights like you did with the rifle, and then, when you're ready, shoot. Just remember that the first time the hammer stops when you're cocking it is half-cocked, and you can't pull the trigger, that's another safety feature, so make sure the hammer is pulled all the way back."

With the barrel still pointed at the ground in front of him, Willie tried using just one thumb to pull the hammer back. It was hard, but he could do it. He raised the pistol, sighted in on the target, and squeezed the trigger. When the pistol fired it sounded a bit louder to him than the rifle had, and the recoil raised it slightly up and to the right in his hand. He hadn't expected that. The rifle recoil had seemed to come straight back against his shoulder.

"Good shot!" Zeke exclaimed from beside him. "Keep holding it up and pointed, then cock it and fire again at the same target. In fact, go ahead and empty the entire cylinder."

Willie fired the remaining four shots and then held the pistol out to Zeke grips first, noting how warm the barrel was in his hand after only being fired five times.

"I'll let you reload it," Zeke told him. "Bring the hammer back to half-cock and leave it there; the trigger mechanism is disengaged, and the cylinder can be turned by hand then. Good. Now open the loading gate on the right side behind the cylinder. You'll see an expended cartridge with a punch mark from the firing pin on the primer in the middle, and if you tilt the pistol up and back, it should slide out of the chamber. If it doesn't, you can use the ejector pin on the underside of the barrel to push it out. Turn the cylinder by hand until all the spent shells are removed."

Willie did so, then knelt and dropped the empty shells on the ground next to the box of live rounds. Zeke continued his instructions. "Now load a new round in the first chamber, revolve the cylinder, and leave the second chamber empty. Load all the rest of the chambers after that, close the loading gate, and pull the hammer all the way back to reengage the cylinder so it turns every time the pistol is cocked. Keep your thumb on the hammer so it doesn't move forward and pull the trigger slowly, then ease the hammer back down with your thumb. That should revolve the cylinder so the empty chamber is under the hammer, and you're ready to shoot again."

Willie was nervous that his thumb might slip as he slowly lowered the hammer but realized it would strike an empty chamber if it did and relaxed a bit. "Let's move back some and have at that second target now," Zeke said.

Willie fired five more rounds at the second target, then looked at Zeke. "Aiming every time sure isn't easy, or fast. How do you get fast?"

"Accuracy first, Willie," Zeke replied. "When the pistol feels like an extension of your hand you'll know that you'll hit what you point it at." He drew his own pistol, turned slightly as he extended his arm, and fired three quick shots at the target as fast as he could cock the hammer. All three shots struck close together in the target, and Willie whistled out loud.

"Why did you turn like that before you fired?" he asked.

"Force of habit, I suppose," Zeke answered. "Standing that way makes me a smaller target."

"A smaller target?"

"Sure. If I went over and turned that board we're shooting at sideways, could you hit the edge of it?"

"I guess I could," Willie answered. "But it wouldn't be easy."

"Exactly," Zeke said. Willie understood. He silently hoped he would never have to face someone shooting at him, and he knew, without being told so, that Zeke had.

Zeke's voice interrupted his thoughts. "I think we're done for today. It will be dark soon, and we don't want to use up all your mother's remaining ammunition. You did very well. I'm impressed."

Willie's chest was still puffed up with pride over Zeke's compliment as they sat on the front porch cleaning the pistol. On their way back to the house, Zeke had stopped off at the barn to get his cleaning kit, and he was instructing Willie on how to use it.

Nana came out of the house with a small pair of sewing scissors. She plucked Zeke's hat off his head and placed it on her rocking chair. "I think those stitches can come out of your head now before it gets too dark out here. Just sit there while I cut them off, and try not to move around too much."

He chuckled. "I'd be afraid to."

He kept on with his instructions to Willie as Nana began snipping the knots off the stitches and sliding the thread out. "When you run the bore brush down the barrel,

178

give it a twist going in and coming back out."

"Hold still!" Nana scolded. "Your hair is already thin on top, and I don't want to cut any more off by accident!"

"Thank you so very much for pointing that out to me," Zeke replied with mock indignation.

"You're a terrible patient," she said. "I noticed you didn't keep that bandage on for more than a few hours after we got home."

"Did you also notice that my hat didn't fit properly with it on? I kept the wound clean, and fresh air helps heal it faster." Zeke hissed in a breath as Nana tugged on a thread. "Ouch! You should really work on your bedside manner, Doctor Miss Nana."

"I told you to hold still!" she said. Willie was trying so hard not to laugh out loud at their exchange that tears rolled down his cheeks, and his nose began to run, making his giggles come out as little snorts.

Rebecca came out of the house just then, wiping her hands on her apron. "What are you two carping at each other about like a couple of magpies out here?"

"Nothing really important," Zeke said.

"We were talking about haircuts now that I've gotten all the stitches out of his head," Nana told her. "I was telling Zeke I would be happy to trim the back of his hair up off his collar after supper. That way he won't go to the Beechers' party looking like a wild man of the woods."

"I was agreeing to a haircut," Zeke added, "as long as she promised not to sneak off and dye my coat black without my permission."

Nana tossed Zeke his hat. "I promise."

CHAPTER 23

"Hold your friends and family close in your heart. Enjoy the good times you have together, and help each other through the bad times."

When Saturday morning arrived, Rebecca and Nana began cooking and baking what they would take to the Beecher gathering the next day, and Willie and Zeke were sent out behind the barn with the bar of Nana's lye soap and towels to clean themselves up. They stopped at the well and drew two buckets of water, one bucket from the well and the other carried from the house. Once safely out of sight by the corral, Zeke stripped off his clothes and emptied a bucket over his head, soaking himself.

He whooped and hopped up and down in place. "Oh! Oh! Cold!" Then he grabbed the bar of soap and lathered his hair and body. Willie noticed that he even had scars on his legs, many as long and ugly as the ones on his back and chest.

Covered in soap suds, Zeke felt around with his foot for the second water bucket. Finding it, he lifted it and dumped it on himself, sputtering. "I'll probably need another bucketful to finish rinsing off! I used too much soap!"

Willie took the empty bucket from Zeke and ran to the well. He tied the rope to it and dropped it down into the water below, then pulled it back up just over half full, untied it, and ran back with it. Zeke poured the fresh water over his head, then grabbed a towel he'd draped over the top corral railing and began to dry off.

"Don't enjoy the spectacle too much, young man," he cautioned, seeing that Willie was laughing as hard as he was. "You're next, and this water is like ice!"

After Zeke got dressed, he refilled the buckets and returned to the spot by the corral. Willie had stripped down, and Zeke dumped the first bucket of water over him. The boy gasped at the chill and tried not to shriek out loud, shivering and jumping around as he rubbed himself with the bar of soap.

"Ready to rinse?" Zeke asked, holding the second bucket ready to pour.

"Yes!" Willie practically shouted. Zeke doused him, then tossed him a towel.

As Willie hurriedly dried off and dressed, Zeke gathered up the buckets, towels, and soap. On their way back to the house, he tied one bucket to the well rope and tossed the wet towels over the clothesline to dry.

"Let's get back in the house quick," Zeke said. "The kitchen should be nice and warm from all the cooking and baking they've been doing in there. Don't let on about how cold the water was unless they notice we've both turned blue because of it."

The inside of the house was indeed quite warm when they entered, a variety of pleasant, mouth-watering aromas hanging in the air like an invisible early morning mist. Willie climbed up to his loft to run a comb through his still-damp hair.

Zeke sat down at the table. "It sure smells good in here. Is there any coffee left?"

Nana checked the pot on the back of the stove. "Yes." She poured him a cup and set it on the table in front of him, then quickly inspected his head injury. "It's healing up nicely," she observed.

"Do I look more civilized since you trimmed my hair last night?" Zeke asked as he picked up the cup and sipped the strong, hot brew.

"Of course," she replied. "But more so when you comb it and shave your face."

Willie climbed down from the loft and joined Zeke at the table. "Can I have some coffee, too?" he asked.

Everybody in the room stopped what they were doing and looked at him quizzically after his unexpected request. Then Rebecca said, "Wouldn't you rather have a fresh brewed cup of tea with a pinch of sugar like always?"

"No, ma'am," Willie responded. "I would like to try some coffee."

"Better put two pinches of sugar in his," Zeke said as Nana moved over to the stove, and Rebecca nodded her consent.

Nana returned with a cupful of coffee, a spoon, and the sugar bowl, setting them down on the table in front of Willie. "I put some sugar in it for you, but if you want more, you can add it. I think there might be another can of condensed milk down in the root cellar if you want to put some of that in also," she added, and Zeke grimaced.

Willie sipped his coffee and made a face, then put it back down on the table and hurriedly added a heaping spoonful of sugar to it.

"It's an acquired taste," Zeke said. "I learned to drink mine without milk or sugar because people were always running out of one or the other or both. As long as there's coffee brewed, I can always have a cup because I don't put anything in it."

"So you're a tough old man inside as well as out?" Nana asked.

Zeke grinned. "Well, I don't know about that, but let's just say I'm still here, and I *do* enjoy my coffee."

"I'm sure glad you're here," said Willie as he took another sip. He still found it somewhat bitter but sweetened enough to suit him. He was unsure if he would ever acquire a taste for it plain, as Zeke said he had done, but was willing to give it a try.

"No place I'd rather be," Zeke replied, smiling over the rim of his cup before taking another sip.

"I'll wager you never thought it would be so dangerous living here, having been shot defending our home and all," Nana said as she moved a pot from the top of the stove to the sideboard.

Zeke looked reflective. "I've been shot before, but sometimes out in the middle of nowhere with nobody around to aid me like you folks did. I'll always be grateful to you all for that."

"Family takes care of family," Rebecca said matter-of-factly as she rinsed and wiped out a pan.

His mother's comment pleased Willie. He had considered Zeke as a welcome member of the family since shortly after the man's arrival and hearing him tell the painful story of his earlier life to them so openly and honestly. He thought of Zeke as a man of kindness, integrity, and courage — someone to grow up and be just like one day, but without having to survive so many injuries in the process.

The conversation among them had slacked off, and the boy found himself watching his mother and grandmother moving around the kitchen with a precision he marveled at. They never once got in each other's way while going about their cooking tasks. The clinking and scraping of pots and pans were the only sounds in the house for many minutes, normal noises he had heard all his life that were comforting and warm to Willie as he sat there.

"Sure does feel cozy, doesn't it?" Zeke said to him. "I've missed that feeling many times over all the years I've spent roaming about."

"You've been to a lot of different places, haven't you?" Willie asked.

"Not as many places as I want to," Zeke said. "But there's still time to see more."

"You're not going to leave us, are you?"

"I won't lie to you, Willie. I will leave someday. Not anytime soon, though."

"I want to go with you!" Willie exclaimed.

"Oh, but you have to stay here for a while yet, my boy. You've got some growing to do still, and the ladies need you around to be of help to them while you do it," Zeke said soothingly.

He winked and grinned at the boy as he turned to speak to the women. "Let us know when you want to go outside and get cleaned up; we'll fill the buckets for you and put them wherever you want."

"You can bring them right into the house so we can warm the water on the stove. We'll use the washtub in here," Rebecca answered.

He choked on a mouthful of coffee. "In here? Why did you send us outside into the cold, then?"

Nana gave a snort of laughter. "Because we couldn't get our cooking and baking done with two naked men prancing around taking up space we needed on the stovetop heating their bath water, that's why."

"Now why didn't I think of that?" Zeke said.

Nana arched her eyebrows. "Because you're a man?"

CHAPTER 24

"Just as day follows the darkest night, so, too, do good events follow the worst of happenings."

Sunday morning dawned fiery red and yellow in the east, with a clear sky overhead and warm breezes from the south that promised a perfect day weatherwise for a gathering with friends and neighbors. Everyone went about their morning routines with a little spring in their step, anticipating an enjoyable day ahead. Willie energetically chopped extra firewood to replenish all that they'd used up the previous day, while Nana hummed a tune as she collected eggs from the chicken coop, and Zeke whistled softly as he fed, watered, and turned Mule and Molly out into the corral. Rebecca, smiling as she worked, was busy in the kitchen making breakfast and packing up all the food they had prepared the day before for the trip over to the Beecher home.

After they ate and the dishes were washed and put up, Zeke and Willie went out to hitch Molly to the wagon and saddle Mule, while Nana and Rebecca moved their cooking and baking, packed carefully in four slatted wooden crates, to the porch to be loaded. As Zeke drove the wagon around to the front of the house, even Molly seemed to prance as if glad to be out of the confines of the barn and corral. Willie led Mule, and she, too, seemed eager to be out on the road in the open air.

While Willie and Zeke loaded the food into the wagon bed, the women changed into their best skirts and white blouses. Rebecca wore a bright blue and white gingham skirt, and Nana donned black muslin. After a quick inspection and adjustments of each other's hair ribbons, they tied on their straw bonnets, picked up their neatly folded knit shawls to wear later if it grew chilly, and were ready to depart.

Willie had already carefully squeezed in among the crates in the back of the wagon. Zeke helped Rebecca up onto the seat, and she took up the reins. Before he could do the same for Nana, she rubbed her hand against his cheek. "That's a pretty close shave. I forgot to check it at breakfast," she

189

said. "Is your hair still combed properly, too?"

Zeke grinned, removed his hat, and tilted his head forward for her to inspect. Satisfied that everything was to her liking, Nana climbed up and settled into the seat while Zeke untied Mule's reins from the rear wagon wheel and swung up into the saddle.

"I'm delighted to see you're not wearing that bloody coat, at least," Nana said.

"It's stuffed in my saddlebag," Zeke replied. "So have no fear that anybody will see it unless I have to put it on. Besides, it's not bloodied anymore, it's just a trifle stained."

"Stained *and* wrinkled?" Nana groused. "They'll think we live like savages out here!"

Zeke let out a laugh and nudged Mule toward the front gate. "Let the adventure begin!"

The ride over to the Beechers' place was pleasant and the mood jovial. They laughed when a family of quail, all in a line, young chicks in the rear, skittered across the road just ahead of the wagon, and Zeke wondered aloud if the birds were hurrying to the gathering also. Soon, the sound of someone sawing at a fiddle could be heard, and the happy squeals and laughter of children at play drifted to their ears on the breeze. They pulled into the property and stopped the wagon at the end of a line of other vehicles over by the barn. Willie noticed his mother looking around as if searching for someone in the crowd of people gathered around the makeshift tables set up in front of the cabin.

"It doesn't appear the Schneiders are here yet. Mary said they were invited," she said with a tinge of disappointment.

"They'll be along," Zeke said as he dismounted and tied Mule to a nearby post.

Tom Beecher approached them, waving and smiling warmly. "The Stevens outfit has arrived bearing more food for the table!" he called out. "I'll help you unload the wagon, then I'll introduce Zeke to the others."

"Help me unload the ladies first. Did everybody accept your invitation?" Zeke asked.

"They sure did!" Beecher replied happily. He'd obviously consumed a good amount of his hard cider before their arrival. Zeke grinned broadly and winked knowingly at Rebecca before helping her down from the wagon seat while Beecher lent Nana a hand dismounting on the other side. Zeke dropped open the tailgate, and Willie handed crates from the back of the wagon to each of them as they came around. Then he jumped down to follow them over to the tables.

"The first two tables are for vittles, savories on the first one where the tin plates and silverware are piled up and sweets on the second one." Beecher pointed. "The last two are for adults and then children to sit at. Cider jugs are lined up in front of the cabin, hard stuff to the right of the door and regular cider on the left. Mary is inside brewing coffee and has hot water for tea. We have pitchers of milk for the little ones, too."

"That's quite a spread." Zeke marveled at the abundance of food as Rebecca and Nana began unpacking the crates and placing their items on the appropriate tables where there was room. "I'll probably be too stuffed to move when this shindig is over."

"Me, too!" Beecher laughed and slapped Zeke on the back, then glanced up as another wagon rattled into the yard. "Ah! I see the Schneiders are finally here! If Mrs. Schneider has brought her homemade pastries, we may have to put a guard on the table to prevent pilfering before supper." He started walking toward where Mr. Schneider had halted his two-seater carriage next to the Stevens wagon.

Zeke glanced over at the adults table

where two men, one holding a violin, were sitting and talking, a cider jug between them. He figured they weren't planning to offer to help carry anything, so he followed Beecher in case his help was needed. When he arrived, the Schneider family had dismounted from the carriage and were busy unloading what they had brought from the rear seat.

"Here's Zeke!" Beecher announced. "If you haven't met him, Mrs. Schneider, allow me to introduce Zeke Smith. He's helping out at the Stevens place!"

Mrs. Schneider was a short, rotund woman with a broad smile and happy manner, curls of silvery-white hair peeking out from beneath her bonnet. Zeke removed his hat and shook the hand she offered, somewhat surprised at the firmness of her grip. "Mr. Zeke Smith!" she said with a slight German accent. "So here is the man who so impressed my Ludwig and Jacob!"

"It's a pleasure, Mrs. Schneider," Zeke replied.

Her smile brightened further. "Oh, please call me Hilde, Zeke. We are good friends now."

"All right, Miss Hilde, what can I help carry?" he said, then put his hat back on and shook hands with her husband and son.

"Good to see you again, gentlemen."

At Mrs. Schneider's direction, the group carried the covered trays of food over to the tables. Mr. Schneider leaned close to Zeke. "I brought my portable writing desk, plus paper, pens, and ink," he said in a low voice. "I left it in the carriage for later. From what Tom told me, we have an important message to send, and I want you to know that I am with you in this endeavor. So is Jacob, wholeheartedly."

"Thank you both," Zeke replied gravely. "This won't be an easy task, and it could very well wind up being dangerous for all of us if we don't stick together."

"I would much rather act now than suffer any more abuse at the hands of this tyrant and his henchmen," Schneider said bluntly as he placed his tray on the dessert table.

By now Hilde Schneider had gone inside the cabin with the rest of the women, where they were warming up the food that needed it on the stove and in the oven. Beecher was sitting with Jacob Schneider and the two other men Zeke had noticed before, so he and Ludwig walked over to join them. Groups of children were happily tossing a ball around or pushing a wooden hoop along the ground with a stick, trying not to let it fall over. Willie was standing off by the shed shyly talking to a dark-haired girl about his own age, in pigtails and an oversized dress that was obviously a hand-me-down.

When Zeke and Ludwig sat down, Beecher jumped up and brought them each a jug of cider. "Boys," he said, "I want to introduce Zeke Smith. He's working out at the Stevens place. This is Stu Jenkins and Pete Phillips." He waved toward the man with the violin and then the other man. "Zeke wants to hear your stories concerning the deaths at the Bidwell place and after."

Zeke rose from his place and shook the hands of each man in turn. As he sat back down, he said to the fiddler, "Why don't you tell your story, Stu? Tom and Pete can agree or disagree with any details as you relate them. I've already heard Tom's version, and I don't know how soon the women will be coming out to gather up the children. The little ones don't need to hear any of it."

CHAPTER 25

"Laugh loud and often when you're happy, and let the tears flow freely when you're sad. Both are just proof that you are still alive inside and out."

Stu Jenkins carefully laid his violin and bow on the table. He reached for his cider jug and took a long drink, then folded his hands in front of him and started talking. He told basically the same tale that Tom Beecher had related to Zeke a few days earlier, but with some added details. "When the marshal told us what direction the raiders went, he said they'd ridden into the woods. He was the one split us up into two groups looking for tracks to follow."

"Did the marshal pick who went with who?" Zeke asked.

"Yep. He did."

When Jenkins had finished, Zeke withdrew an item wrapped in cloth from his pants pocket and placed it on the table.

"Is this what Tom found near the bodies?" he asked as he opened the wrapping.

At the sight of the Apache necklace, Jenkins and Phillips both nodded. Zeke rewrapped it and carefully returned it to his pocket, then turned to Ludwig Schneider, who was seated beside him. "That's the incident we need you to write up for these fellows to sign, the alleged Indian raid at the Bidwell place. Feel free to add any questionable happenings in town that the marshal or his deputies were involved in, and you're welcome to sign it also."

Schneider pulled out his handkerchief and wiped his brow. "That terrible day is seared into my mind," he said softly.

Across the table, Jacob reached out and patted his father's hand. "Papa is a man of peace," he told the others. "He was a young soldier in the Austrian-Prussian War many years ago, and any reminder of violence resulting in death still disturbs him greatly. I'll make a statement for us and sign it."

"We're all agreed, then?" Zeke asked, and the men all nodded. "Good! We'll ride over to the county seat as soon as we can and deliver the statement to the sheriff in person."

"I can't make that long a ride," Jenkins

answered sadly. "I was chopping down a tree with a dull axe last week and it bounced back and hit me in the leg. Hasn't healed up enough."

"Jacob should stay here to keep an eye on his parents and the situation," Beecher said. "So I guess it's up to you, me, and Phillips, Zeke. When do you want to leave?"

"Tomorrow, if we're all sober," Zeke replied.

Beecher chuckled. "No chance of that. Maybe the day after?"

Several minutes later, the women emerged from the cabin carrying platters of warmed food and called everyone to the table as they put them down. The children rushed in so their mothers could line them up, fill their plates, and walk them over to the children's table while the men stood and waited their turn. After the children were all situated, the men picked up plates, knives, and forks, then filed down each side of the food table filling their plates with a variety of savory meats, breads, and vegetables. As the men began to seat themselves, the women filled their own plates and came to join them. Some couples said grace over their food, while others dug right in, and the feast was underway amid much friendly conversation and laughter.

Tom Beecher stood and raised his jug high, shouting over the happy voices and the clinking of silverware on plates around him, "Here's to good friends and better times!"

A chorus of voices repeated his toast, followed immediately by raucous laughter as he sat down without looking behind himself and missed his chair. He landed on the ground, still holding his jug, with his feet high in the air. He looked dumbfounded for a second, then chuckled as he reached up and took his plate from the table and set it on his lap.

"I better finish my meal down here. It'll be safer for me that way," he announced loudly.

Mary rose from her place, took his plate, put it back up on the table, and helped Tom stand up. "Always playing the fool, aren't you, Thomas Beecher? Sit down and behave yourself now!" she mock-scolded him.

Nana, who had seated herself next to Zeke, elbowed him in the ribs. "See what that hard cider does to a person? But you already know that from previous experience, don't you?"

"That's why I replaced mine with a jug of regular cider when nobody in the food line was looking," he answered with a sly smile.

"Prove that!" she demanded, so he slid his jug over to her. She sniffed it, then leaned over to whisper in his ear, "Now you've gone and spoiled all my fun, Zeke! Instead of watching you get drunk, I have to watch Rebecca batting her eyelashes and smiling coyly at young Jacob Schneider all afternoon."

"Try watching Willie and the pretty, dark-haired girl with the pigtails," he replied, and she turned around to glance over at the children's table.

"I hadn't noticed them before," she said. "That's the Phillips's granddaughter, Ruth. She came to live with them when her parents died of a sickness. It's good to see her socializing at last. She was in a dark humor for a very long time."

"Willie will make a good impression on her." Zeke got up from the table with his plate in hand. "I'm going back for seconds. Can I bring you anything?"

"I took enough food the first time around," Nana answered. "But another corn muffin and a dollop of butter would be nice."

When Zeke joined the line for second helpings he stood behind Hilde Schneider, who was holding two plates. As they neared the table, she turned and smiled up at him.

"I'm getting more for Ludwig and me; all this fresh air has given us both quite an appetite. We hardly ever get out of the house or store most days. This outing is certainly a welcome change."

"I'm going to take some of what I didn't have the first time through," Zeke answered as he eyed the items on the table, trying to decide what he wanted to sample next.

"Leave room for dessert," she reminded him. "I spent a day and a half over a hot oven baking special treats for this day."

"What did you make?" he asked.

"Nothing really that hard," she answered. "Just bienenstich, kolachi, baumkuchen, and for the little ones pfeffernuesse, lebkuchen, and springerle." Noticing the quizzical look on Zeke's face, she quickly added, "Cakes and cookies. When I'm ready to uncover them, I'll put together a plate of everything just for you to taste."

"I would really appreciate that, Miss Hilde," he said with a smile as he started down the food table behind her, filling his plate as he walked. He made a mental note to be sure to have some of Miss Nana's vinegar pie along with Miss Hilde's cakes and cookies or he would never hear the end of it. When they returned to their seats, Mrs. Schneider leaned over and spoke to her husband in German. He nodded in approval, and she slid his refilled plate in front of him as she took her seat beside him. Zeke sat down beside Nana, handed her the corn muffin and butter she had requested, and started to eat again.

Twenty or so minutes later, Mary Beecher stood and looked around at her guests. "Has everybody finished their meal? We'll open up the dessert table now. I put out fresh plates and silverware there. Who wants coffee or tea?"

Zeke raised his hand. "Coffee here, please!" he answered loudly as others voiced their preferences, and the women rose from their places to either go to the dessert table and uncover the treats or bring their excited children over to line up and make their choices. Tom went into the cabin and returned with a large wooden tub, which he put on the ground at one end of the dessert table.

"Dirty dishes and silverware in here, if you will!" he announced.

Nana spoke to Rebecca and pointed to Willie and Ruth in line, the boy walking behind the girl carrying two plates as she placed items on them. When it was the men's turn, Zeke noticed Tom talking to Ludwig as they stood together in line behind him. After he took a piece of Nana's pie, Mrs. Schneider handed him the promised plateful of her contributions, and he walked back to his place with Beecher.

"After dessert," Tom told him, "Ludwig, Jacob, and I will slip into the shed with his writing materials, and I'll help him write up our paper."

"Be easy with him if he gets upset again," Zeke replied. "I've seen a few former soldiers who were bothered by memories of what they experienced."

"I'll be mindful of that," Tom said seriously as he sat down.

Out on the road near the Beecher farmstead, hidden from view by trees, Deputy Joe Spinks quietly mounted his horse. He turned the animal back toward town and silently rode away.

CHAPTER 26

"When your course is set, stick to it no matter what obstacles you may encounter."

After everyone finished eating their fill, many having gone back to the dessert table more than once, Mary brought out cups, the coffee pot, and hot water for tea to those that had requested it. Stu Jenkins took up his violin and played a medley of lively tunes while those who knew the words to them sang along. The children soon went back to their games, and the women began to move around the tables, engaging in pleasant conversation and complimenting each other's cooking and baking skills, reciting their recipes when asked. Nobody took any notice of Tom Beecher and the Schneider men going out to the carriage, retrieving the portable writing desk, and entering the shed together.

Within half an hour, Beecher emerged

alone and walked over to whisper in Phillips's ear, who rose from the table and ambled toward the shed.

Tom sat down next to Zeke. "You'll have to sign the document also," he said. "We included the incident at the Stevens place where you were wounded, that the deputies took part in at the marshal's instigation."

"Happy to oblige." Zeke sipped his coffee and ate his last cookie, the name of which he couldn't pronounce if his life depended on it, but that he found delicious nevertheless. After several minutes, Phillips exited the shed and spoke briefly to Jenkins, who put down his violin, limped over to the shed, and entered the small building.

"Mr. Schneider handled it very well," Beecher said quietly. "He put down the written story mostly from memory without any difficulty at all, although he questioned me on exact details a few times before putting pen to paper."

"I'm glad he agreed to do this for us," Zeke replied gravely. "His involvement adds a lot more credence to the complaint. He and Jacob are showing their grit by joining us. I wish we had thought to ask some of the other bullied merchants to come in on it."

When Jenkins emerged from the shed a

few minutes later, Zeke walked over to it. As he closed the door behind him, it took his eyes about a minute to adjust to the dimness inside; the flickering lamp on the workbench was obviously running low on oil. Ludwig Schneider sat on a tall stool in front of the workbench holding a pen. Jacob stood behind him. The portable writing desk rested atop the bench's gouged and scarred surface. Several sheets of paper were spread out on the hinged, slanted desktop, and an ornate inkwell sat beside the desk.

Ludwig Schneider held the pen out to Zeke. "With your signature, Mr. Smith, the die is cast," he said solemnly.

"I'll read it first," Zeke replied.

"Of course." Schneider's voice trembled slightly as he gathered up the pages, four in all, and handed them to Zeke. "There is room on the last page for all the signatures."

Zeke turned his back to the lamp and held the pages up in the dancing light that glowed from over his shoulder. Everything seemed to be there in the elder Schneider's crisp, flowing handwriting: the site of the Bidwell massacre and who was there after it, the discovery of damning evidence at the scene, the pursuit of an invisible enemy amid misgivings that all was not right with the situation, and the suspicious death of

206

Will Stevens. Schneider had also written of property owners forced to make improvements to increase land values before sudden bank foreclosures, and merchants in town being pressured into renting unneeded bank properties or do business in a certain way. The document ended with the nighttime raid on the Stevens place that resulted in Zeke's injury. The few lines on the fourth page attested to the truthfulness of the statement and requested an immediate investigation by higher authorities. The other men's signatures took up the space below.

Zeke smiled and took the pen from Ludwig, dipped it in the inkwell, and wrote his name under Jacob Schneider's.

"This is perfect," he said as he handed the pen back and blew softly on the wet ink. "You are an intelligent and brave man. Thank you for helping us. I'm proud to know you and your family."

"No, no," Ludwig protested as he rose from the stool and extended his hand. "Tom told me that this idea to seek legal help to redress our grievances was all your doing! You have taken a flock of sheep and given us the courage of a pride of lions! We should be thanking you!"

"Don't celebrate just yet," Zeke cautioned

them as he shook Ludwig's hand and then Jacob's. "If this doesn't work out there will be hell to pay with Marshal Seegern and his bullies still in charge."

"We'll be sharpening our claws, just in case," Jacob answered.

Ludwig took the document back from Zeke, flipped through the pages to make sure they were in the correct order, then carefully folded them in thirds, withdrew an envelope from the desk, slipped the folded papers inside, and handed the envelope back to Zeke. He capped the inkwell, raised the lid of the writing desk, and placed it inside along with the pen. Jacob picked it up while Zeke blew out the lamp and they left the shed together.

Outside, the women were clearing leftovers from the tables, happily chatting among themselves and exchanging portions to take home of whatever foodstuffs that remained. While Jacob carried the writing desk back to the carriage, Zeke and Ludwig returned to the tables and offered to help, an offer that was gently refused on the grounds that they would just be underfoot and in the way. Ludwig sat down while Zeke picked up his nearly empty cup and searched for the coffee pot. Jenkins was back at his seat playing serene, calming music on his violin.

Nana came up to Zeke just as he spotted the coffee pot on the end of the dessert table and started toward it. "What were you all doing, sneaking in and out of Beecher's shed earlier?" she asked. "I watched you boys as I stood in line with some other ladies waiting to use the outhouse."

Zeke lifted the errant pot and poured himself a fresh cupful. He was glad to note that it was still warm. "We wrote up and signed a complaint about the marshal and the way he runs things around here, asking for an investigation. We're going to deliver it to the county sheriff in person, probably the day after tomorrow." He tapped his shirt, where he'd safely tucked the written statement in its envelope. "I've got it here. You can read it later at home if you like."

"It's about time someone did something!" Nana exclaimed. "Just don't sweat all over it so it's unreadable."

As the women finished their work, Tom and Mary Beecher began bringing buckets of heated water out of the cabin and dumping them into the tub of dirty dishes. That action silently signaled the guests to start packing up their wagons with their empty plates, platters, and any leftovers not given away. Zeke, Nana, and Rebecca loaded their wagon while Willie helped Ruth and the Phillips family load theirs, then lent a hand to the others with whatever remained to be carried. Tom, Mary, and the Beecher children joined the assembly, and goodbye hugs and handshakes were exchanged all around.

"Mary and I just want to thank you all for coming today," Tom told them. "Thank you also, ladies, for leaving us a large portion of your leftovers. We'll have the plumpest, most well-fed children in the territory!"

"Which they'll burn right off in a few days of play," Mary added.

Tom turned to Zeke. "Phillips will ride by your place on Tuesday morning early, and you both can come get me," he murmured. "We can make it to the county seat well before dark if we don't dally on the road."

The families got into their wagons. Zeke and Jacob helped Ludwig and Hilde Schneider up onto the front seat of their carriage, and Jacob hopped up on the rear seat where the empty platters were piled. Tom stood in front of their team of horses and pushed the animals' chests gently when Ludwig pulled lightly on the reins, a signal to back up. The well-trained team responded, and the wagon was soon turned and heading for the road. Hilde waved to everyone as they left. Once the Schneider carriage was gone, there was just enough room for Rebecca to turn Molly and move the Stevens wagon out. Heeding Nana's earlier admonition, Zeke removed the envelope from his shirt and tucked it in one of his saddlebags before he untied and mounted Mule.

"Aren't you forgetting someone?" he asked Rebecca as he rode up beside her. She glanced into the back of the wagon.

"Willie!" she said, sounding startled to discover he was not there. She pulled Molly to a halt. Willie was still in the Beechers' yard, standing at the Phillips wagon talking to Ruth before she got on board. Ruth suddenly leaned forward and kissed Willie on the cheek, then bounded up onto her family's wagon.

Red-faced, but grinning widely, Willie ran to the Stevens wagon and leapt into the back among the crates.

"Drive!" he shouted.

CHAPTER 27

"Knowledge can sometimes be painful, but unanswered questions are always maddening. Learn all you can, whenever you can."

At home, later that night at the lamplit kitchen table, Zeke let Rebecca and Nana read the letter to the sheriff. Willie sat there observing his mother and grandmother. Their faces showed surprise, then anger, followed by grief as silent tears welled up and rolled down their cheeks. When they had finished reading, Zeke slid the papers across the table to Willie.

"It's time you knew," he said gravely.

Willie picked up the letter with trembling hands, curious but also terrified of what he was about to read. He knew they were all watching him, so he tried to be brave as he absorbed the words. It was harder to breathe right with each sentence he read, and he tried mightily not to scream or burst into tears as he reached the end. He put the papers down and slid them back to Zeke.

"I want to kill them for what they did!" he blurted out, his voice breaking.

Zeke's voice was calm as he refolded the letter and returned it to the envelope. "I know you do, Willie, and I don't blame you. But you have to trust the law to handle it the right way. Without laws to protect us, we're no better than a howling pack of wild animals."

"But they're supposed to *be* the law, and they killed my father!" Willie clenched his fists and began to sob.

Rebecca rose from her chair and came around the table, wrapped him in her arms, and hugged him tightly. "There are liars, cheats, and sometimes murderers in every walk of life, Son," she whispered gently. "They all get caught at it eventually and face a day of reckoning."

"Their day of reckoning starts right here." Zeke tapped the envelope on the table in front of him. "I give you my promise here and now, Willie, that they will pay a terrible price for their evil deeds. I'll see to it."

The Stevens family sat at the table, talking in hushed tones, weeping and comforting each other, for another hour after Zeke had gone out to the barn for the night. Finally, Nana suggested they all try to get some sleep. After climbing up to the loft and crawling into bed, Willie comforted himself with the memory of Ruth's tender kiss on his cheek earlier that day. He eventually fell into a fitful slumber punctuated with nightmares of faceless demons firing guns at him.

Early the next day, Zeke had just finished getting dressed when he heard the barn door open slowly. He silently drew his pistol and held it down at his side, thumb on the hammer, waiting in the shadows as a widening shaft of morning light snaked along the floor. Molly and Mule stirred nervously in their stalls.

"Zeke? Are you awake?"

The horse and mule softly whinnied at the familiar sound of the boy's voice. Zeke relaxed and holstered his pistol.

"Yes, Willie." He put on his hat, stepped out into the center of the barn, and walked toward the door.

"Does it hurt bad to be shot?" Willie asked as Zeke approached.

Zeke halted. "Now that I think of it," he replied, "I can't say it does at first. It feels more like somebody picked up a big stick,

214

swung it as hard as they could, and hit you with it. You feel the impact, but your body numbs the spot right away while it tries to figure out what happened. It stays numb for a bit. Pain comes later."

Willie was silent for a minute. Then he asked, "Do you think my pa felt any pain?"

Zeke let out a breath. "Judging by what was told to me, I'm sure he didn't feel any at all."

Willie's voice cracked. "I'm glad of that," he said.

Zeke rested his hand on the boy's shoulder. "Let's not dwell on it now. We have chores to do before breakfast, and we better get to them."

While Willie began his morning task at the woodpile, Zeke drew water from the well, poured it into an empty bucket he'd brought from the barn, and took it to the corral to dump it into the water trough. He had to make three trips to finish filling the trough, and then he went back into the barn to give Molly and Mule their morning portion of fresh hay and put scoops of oats into their feed bins. That done, he brought a rake and shovel from the tool room and placed them in the rickety wooden wheelbarrow just inside the rear barn door, in preparation for mucking out the stalls later.

When he emerged from the barn, Willie was just carrying an armload of split wood and kindling into the house and Nana was following him in with a basket of fresh eggs from the chicken coop. Looking at the sky, where grey clouds were gathered on the horizon and rays of sunlight shot up through them like shining spears, Zeke smiled at the normalcy of it all, even in the face of the looming whirlwind he knew was to come.

Breakfast that morning was somber, everyone lost in their own thoughts. Nana finally broke the silence. "When are you heading out to deliver that letter, Zeke?"

"Early tomorrow," he answered. "Phillips is stopping by here, and Beecher will join us on the way."

"I'll pack you a lunch," Rebecca said. "Don't let Tom Beecher bring any of his homemade happy juice, or you'll never get there." They all laughed at that, lightening the mood somewhat.

"Can I go with you?" Willie inquired.

"I think it best that you stay here," Zeke replied. "Someone has to be here to protect the ladies against any harm while I'm away. I trust you to handle that task as well as I could, now that you're a crack shot. I should be back by sometime Wednesday at the latest."

"I'll bake you a cake!" Nana said with a wry smile. "So you'll be sure to hurry back!"

"You can count on it!" Zeke exclaimed.

After breakfast, Zeke went back to the barn to finish the chores. Willie tried to concentrate on his morning lessons but found it impossible to do so. An exasperated Rebecca finally ended the lessons and told him to go out and help Zeke, an order he gladly obeyed.

The barn was empty when Willie arrived, and he could see one stall had already been cleaned. Looking out the stall window, he saw Zeke dumping the wheelbarrow on the manure pile located away from the barn near the tree line. He picked up the rake that Zeke had left behind and started mucking out the one stall left to clean out. Zeke returned to the barn a few minutes later with the empty wheelbarrow and smiled broadly.

"Well, this is a surprise, my boy. Thank you for the helping hand," he said. "I had thought you might have forgotten how to do this chore since I arrived and took it over."

Willie stopped raking and leaned on the tool handle. "Ma and me used to do this, but there was only Molly's stall to do then.

217

Nana cleans out the chicken coop."

"The chicken coop," Zeke mused. "I hadn't thought to include that in my chores. Maybe I should start."

"Nana would be pleased," Willie said. "The manure pile is a long walk for her sometimes, so she skips a few days in a row."

"We'll clean that out next. Finish your raking, and I'll shovel."

When they moved out to the chicken coop, Zeke looked inside, while Willie prevented any birds from escaping out the door with the rake. Shovel in hand, Zeke made a face. "How can such small critters create so much dung? It's everywhere in here!"

"Get what you can out!" Willie said, waving the rake back and forth in the half-open doorway. "I don't know if I can keep them in there much longer!"

Zeke scraped the shovel along the floor of the coop three times, pulling out as much waste as he could onto the ground by the door before hurriedly pushing it closed. After shoveling it onto the wheelbarrow atop the horse droppings, they headed out to the manure pile.

Willie saw that Zeke's nose was running, and tears glistened on his cheeks. "Smells pretty bad, doesn't it?" he said, giggling.

"I don't think I've smelled anything worse, unless you count something dead that's lain out in the sun for a few days. Miss Nana must have a special way of doing that job without fainting from the stench." Zeke dumped the wheelbarrow, then coughed and spat, "I'll need that long ride tomorrow just to clear my head!"

CHAPTER 28

"When things look bleak, hang on a bit longer and try a little harder. The situation will likely improve, and if it doesn't, at least you tried your best."

Willie and Zeke spent the remainder of the day greasing the wagon wheels. After they pushed the wagon out from under the lean-to, Zeke loosened each wheel nut in the hub, then put his shoulder under the side of the wagon and lifted it as high as he could while Willie wrestled the heavy wheel off and coated the axle shaft thoroughly, using a large wooden spoon to dip up from a bucket of axle grease. When Willie slid the wheel back on, Zeke lowered the wagon and retightened the nut. They repeated the process with all four wheels, with longer rest periods in between as their strength began to fade with time and effort. During their rests, Zeke made sure Willie hadn't gotten any grease on his clothes because Willie's mother would have their hides if he did and she couldn't wash it out.

"For a small wagon, it sure isn't light," Zeke panted when they'd finished the last wheel and rolled the wagon back under its shelter. After their exertions, Zeke and Willie agreed they had no wish to be called to do some other chore if they were spotted being idle, so they lazed around inside the barn for the rest of the afternoon, rearranging the tool room until it was time to eat.

That evening during dinner Willie related the chicken coop story and everyone had a good laugh at Zeke's discomfort during the cleaning incident.

"I never clean the coop out during the early morning when I can't leave the door wide open," Nana said. "I don't let them out to roam just after dawn, but later in the morning, and I shoo them back in before dusk. That's when the coyotes and foxes are out hunting a quick meal, and we don't want those critters hanging around the place waiting for one. I collect the eggs at sunrise as quick as I can, and I keep a perfumed handkerchief in my apron pocket to hold over my nose."

"I'll remember that when I finish the job

after I get back," Zeke noted. "I do think I'll forego the perfumed handkerchief, though, and use a bandanna instead."

The next morning, before the first rays of the rising sun lightened the eastern sky, Zeke had already risen, dressed, and was mounted on Mule, waiting on the road outside the front gate for Pete Phillips to arrive. He held the collar of his coat closed against the predawn chill and chuckled to himself, remembering how he had convinced Miss Nana he had carelessly stuffed the coat into his saddlebags when he had, in fact, neatly folded it before placing it inside. It still amused him how she had howled in embarrassment at the thought of him wearing wrinkled clothes in public as a bad reflection on her homemaking skills. He glanced back at the house and saw light bloom inside as lamps were lit, just as he heard the steady clip-clop of a horse's hooves approaching. Mule caught the horse's scent and snorted, answered from the darkness by a whinny.

"That you, Phillips?" Zeke called out softly, his right hand drifting to his pistol grip.

"Who else would be out for a ride in the cold and dark, when he could be home in a cozy, warm bed?" came the reply as Phillips's mounted figure took shape out of the gloom.

"At least the sun should just be coming up by the time we get to Beecher's," Zeke observed. "Maybe we'll have time to stop in for coffee; I'm missing my morning cup today."

They rode along side by side as the sky and surrounding environment began to lighten and details of the familiar landscape became more visible to them. As the first rays of the sun pierced the trees, mourning doves began cooing, and other awakening birds of varying species joined in with their own vocalizations. The riders approached the Beecher place and saw Tom out on the road, mounted and ready to join them.

He waved as they rode up to him. "It's going to be a nice day for a ride with friends!" he called out.

"I just pray we're not making a long journey for nothing," Phillips said as the three horsemen, riding abreast, started out on the road to town.

"You don't think we're on a fool's errand, do you, Zeke?" Beecher asked.

"I think this is your best course of action right now, or I wouldn't have suggested it," Zeke replied. "If you fight back against being ridden roughshod over without being organized, the marshal can claim to have the law on his side and pick you off one at a time. But if you enlist the law in your cause first, you stand a good chance of winning your case."

"Three knights on a quest for justice!" Phillips announced with a wry chuckle.

Less than an hour later they rode through the town of Pleasant Grove, its streets deserted and shops yet to be opened for the new day. The only person in sight this early was Sheila Bacron, just stepping through the doorway of the boardinghouse she ran, broom in hand, to sweep the wooden sidewalk in front of her establishment.

Sheila Bacron watched intently as the three riders passed through town. She noted who they were, and the road they took out of Pleasant Grove. She took the time to carefully sweep her porch and the boardwalk, then leaned the broom against the wall and hurried across the street to the marshal's office.

After a few minutes inside, she emerged and walked back to the boardinghouse. Time to cook breakfast for her boarders before she roused them from their slumbers.

The three riders continued on their way.

They passed small farms very much like their own, spaced far apart on either side of the road, and showing more signs of early morning activity than their neighbors inside the town limits who were just now climbing out of their beds. Roosters crowed, dogs barked, pigs grunted, horses whinnied, and an occasional raised human voice could be heard as they passed by the increasingly isolated farmsteads. Those familiar sounds, too, faded away in the distance as they traveled on through the yet to be tamed forest.

Tom Beecher drew in a deep breath and exhaled slowly. "Spring is my favorite of the four seasons!"

"There are only three seasons up here," Phillips said.

"Just three?" Zeke asked.

"Of course." Phillips chuckled. "Planting season, swatting flies season, and harvest season!"

"Such is our life," Beecher agreed.

"I can think of worse occupations than working the soil and raising a family," Zeke said wistfully.

"Do you have a family somewhere, Zeke?" Beecher asked.

"No. I guess I never had the time to get domesticated and settle down. There was a young lady back in Texas, though. I do wonder what happened to her from time to time."

When the sun stood directly overhead, they stopped where a small stream flowed beside the road to water their animals and stretch their legs. The landscape was changing now, rising and falling gently with more open, grassy areas between the trees and solitary rock formations scattered about as if carelessly dropped there by some giant hand. Zeke removed the canvas bag, hanging by its drawstrings from his saddle horn, that contained the lunch Miss Rebecca had given him. Inside it he found four, plump homemade biscuits wrapped in cloth, each containing a slice of cooked venison slathered with sugar syrup. Beecher also had a prepared lunch, fished from his saddlebag, of fried egg sandwiches made with thick slices of bread. Phillips had forgotten his lunch, so they shared some of theirs with him. When Beecher snagged a canteen that hung from his saddle, Zeke eyed him suspiciously.

"Do you have firewater cider in there?" he asked.

Beecher laughed. "No, my friend, I don't," he replied. "I need my wits about me today because we have important work to do. Do you want to taste it?"

"I trust your word."

"Then let's be on our way!" Phillips said. "We can't be more than a few hours or so from our destination."

"Two at the most." Beecher mounted his horse. "We should start seeing signs of civilization pretty soon."

CHAPTER 29

"Even the most mundane tasks can yield useful results. Nothing that affects your life, or the lives of others, should ever be considered boring."

County Sheriff Bill Mulvenon eased himself back in his chair, the desk in front of him piled high with official papers he had been poring over and rubbed his tired eyes. It was days like this, trapped indoors by boring office duties, that made him miss riding the hills and valleys of his youth enforcing the laws of the rough-and-tumble territory. As he stretched out his arms and swiveled his head from side to side, easing a crick in his neck, someone knocked on his office door. "Come ahead," he groaned, dreading another delivery of paperwork to be attended to.

Deputy Jimmy Ciglan opened the door and poked his head inside. "There's three fellas out here who wants to talk with you, Sheriff," he announced. "They says it's real important."

"Tell them to come in, as long as there's no paperwork involved," he replied.

Ciglan threw open the door and stepped aside to allow the three visitors to enter the office. "Sorry, Sheriff," the lead man said as he walked in. Lean of build but not especially tall, he had pale-blue eyes and wore a Colt .45 in a worn leather gun belt. He carried an envelope in one hand. "There is some small amount of paperwork involved, I'm afraid."

The sheriff sighed as he rose from his chair. "Well, it's too late for me to duck out the back door now." He extended his hand across his desk. "I'm Sheriff Mulvenon."

The man shook hands with him. "I'm Zeke Smith, and this is Tom Beecher and Pete Phillips. We're just in from Pleasant Grove with an urgent matter that requires your attention."

Beecher and Phillips shook hands with the sheriff as well and then pulled over chairs that were lined up against the wall opposite the desk and sat down. As the deputy closed the office door behind them, Zeke handed the envelope to the lawman. "Our situation is outlined in this document. If you'll read it, Sheriff, then we can talk."

The sheriff sat, opened the envelope, withdrew and read the pages. Several minutes passed while he read them, punctuated with an occasional raised eyebrow, a frown, and a muttered, "Oh," and, "Hmm." When he finished reading, he set the letter down, leaned back in his chair, and tapped his fingertips together across his chest. Zeke and the others seated in front of him exchanged glances and waited with eager anticipation for him to speak.

"I have to tell you gentlemen that this is not the first time I've heard the Apache raid story, and I find it unsettling, to say the least," Mulvenon said at last. "Some time ago a fellow named Holly or Holland passing through town told the same story to our local storekeeper, who passed it on to me."

"Hollis?" Beecher offered.

"That's the name!" Mulvenon exclaimed. "Hollis didn't wind up settling near here, but moved on to parts unknown, so I was unable to question him concerning the incident. Now I have this signed document, which, I assume, you've all affixed your names to as witnesses to the events listed?"

"We're all here but the Schneiders, but we can vouch for their truthfulness," Zeke said. He dug into his pants pocket and brought out the cloth-wrapped necklace Tom Beecher had given to him for safekeeping. He unwrapped it and laid it on the desk in front of the sheriff. "Here is the evidence found at the Bidwell place. Maybe you recognize it?"

Mulvenon studied it intently. "I certainly do know this type of necklace. It's worn by young Apache girls, is it not?"

"It is," Zeke replied as Beecher and Phillips gaped at him. "They wear it at the ceremony when they are ushered into womanhood. No Apache warrior would possess such a thing, let alone drop it at the site of a raid. One of the marshal's deputies has quite a collection of Apache and other tribal artifacts from when he served in the militia."

He gestured at the leather thongs used to tie it around the neck. "You'll notice those have been cut, and there's dried blood on the necklace as well. Someone cut this off an Apache girl. Whether she was alive or dead at the time I don't know, but I would guess she was dead or she would have fought hard to keep it."

The sheriff nodded, then leaned forward, elbows on his desk and a somber expression on his face. "Now let me tell you a story of my own. When this tale first came to me, I checked my records from around that time.

I require town marshals in my county to file monthly reports with me about what goes on in their jurisdictions. None of your Marshal Seegern's reports mentioned any Apache raid that resulted in deaths. The reports were, in fact, quite bland — just bank foreclosures enforced, taxes collected, and drunk and disorderly arrests. I can't imagine he would have forgotten such a violent incident, so I can only suspect he didn't want it to be widely known outside the community he could control."

"Because he was behind the whole thing!" Phillips said. "I knew it!"

"We all knew it, but we were too scared to say so," Beecher said sadly. "It took Zeke here to bring the truth into the light and help us stand up for it . . . and for ourselves."

"You had families to consider," Zeke said. "You needed to keep them safe from harm. You also helped the Stevens family survive because of what happened, even though you knew Marshal Seegern might make you pay for that if he found out about it. That sort of commitment to what's right is real bravery in my book."

"Allow me to offer you gentlemen a proposition," the sheriff said. "I'm a bit short-handed on deputies right now, and I need some time to round up a circuit court judge so I can come and conduct a proper inquiry into just how Marshal Seegern runs your town. From the sound of things, a bank auditor isn't a bad idea, either. Would you three accept appointment as special deputy sheriffs to return to Pleasant Grove and keep a lid on things until I arrive? Quietly, of course. And I should tell you, there won't be any pay in it. But it's a job that needs doing. What do you say?"

The three men sat in stunned silence. Then Zeke shook his head and cleared his throat. "Tom and Pete here are good choices, and I will aid them all I can," he said. "But the last time I wore a badge I tarnished it badly. I'm still trying to make up for that and a few other sins of my past."

Beecher and Phillips stared at him, while Mulvenon grinned. "I knew you had the look and manner of a lawman! I figured you were one, or had been, the minute you walked in here!"

Zeke nodded with a trace of a smile, which quickly faded. "I still can't accept your offer."

"Let me try to persuade you, Mr. Smith," Mulvenon said, his voice serious now. "Whatever wrong you may have done in the past — and I won't ask — what better way to atone for it than to pin on the badge again and do the *right* thing?"

"I've spent years trying to do the right thing without the badge," Zeke answered. "For the most part I have succeeded."

"So, why don't you tell me your story and let me decide?"

Zeke fell deathly silent for a moment. Then he sighed deeply. "It's not something I've ever told anyone except the Stevens family, and I left the worst of it out. If I tell you the whole of it, it must never leave this room, not ever."

CHAPTER 30

"Always tell the truth, even if it'll cost you. The cost of lying, even by silence, is almost always greater."

The three men nodded in agreement, and Zeke began. "I was the marshal of Rio Bonita, a quiet little town in south Texas. A group of cowboys rode in one day with a small herd of horses they had stolen in Mexico. They put them up at the livery corral and visited the local saloon, and sometime during their carousing they decided to rob the saloon along with the general store. A store clerk was shot and wounded during the robbery, and the cowboys ran to the livery to retrieve their herd and mounts. I came out of my office at the sound of gunfire just as they were stampeding their herd down the main street, shooting into the buildings and whooping like wild savages as they rode by."

He drew a steadying breath, knowing what came next. "I saw a pregnant woman in the middle of the street, frozen in terror as the horses bore down on her. They rode her down and trampled her as I watched. I mounted my horse and took out after them. I never even bothered to stop and help the woman lying in the street. Catching those outlaws was all I could think of, and rendering aid to that poor woman would have slowed me down. I've always regretted that heartless decision.

"I pursued them for miles out into the rolling hills. Their dust cloud was easy to follow, since they were too greedy to abandon their herd. But I knew the country and realized they would find it hard to keep the herd together in the scrub brush that grew over the hilltops and in the small valleys. I took a circular route around them to cut them off following a nearby river, where the terrain was flatter and less hilly. One man on a horse doesn't raise much dust on grassy ground, and pretty soon I figured I was ahead of them. I dismounted in a stand of trees and waited, rifle at the ready, as I watched their dust cloud draw nearer."

A chair creaked as Tom Beecher stirred, but he didn't say anything. Zeke kept his gaze on the edge of the sheriff's desk as he went on. "They came in view before long. They had the horses under control by then, two riders on either side of the herd, one rider in the lead, and the other two following behind. As they drew abreast of where I was hiding, I could hear them laughing and joking among themselves.

"Something snapped inside me at that sound. I stepped out into the open and raised my rifle, aiming at the lead rider. I shouted no warning, no order to throw up their hands or that they were under arrest, I just shot the man out of the saddle and then turned my rifle on the riders behind the herd. As the horses bolted and scattered, I aimed and fired as fast as I could cock the lever. Two of the horse thieves went down, and the last pair opened fire on me. Their horses were spooked, so most of their shots went wild, but three shots struck me as far as I know. I was hit in the chest near my right shoulder, in my left thigh, and a third bullet grazed my head above my ear. I managed to stay standing somehow and shoot those men. Took my last bullets. I didn't know 'til then that my rifle wasn't fully loaded."

Pete Phillips gave a low whistle. "Lucky," he said softly.

"Not for them." Zeke gripped his hands

together. "I dropped the empty rifle and hobbled forward to where their bodies lay. Three of them were still moving. I drew my pistol and executed the wounded, then fell to the ground unconscious from loss of blood amid my victims. I had sworn to uphold justice, but instead I took bloody revenge."

Finally able to do so, Zeke looked up at the sheriff. "I don't know how long I lay there before two vaqueros from a nearby ranchero arrived on the bloody scene and rescued me. They found my horse tied up in the trees, lifted me into the saddle, and led me away from the site of the carnage I had created. Neither of them thought I would live long enough to reach the hacienda. But I did live, and, when I was healed enough to leave, I put the badge I had disgraced away and never wore it again. I've been sort of a wanderer ever since."

The room was silent for many minutes. Zeke rubbed his eyes with his thumb and forefinger, reluctant to look at the others as each man mulled over what he had just told them. Then Sheriff Mulvenon cleared his throat. "Well, Mr. Smith, that was quite a confession, and I truly hope you feel better for it. I see no wrong in what you did. When we pin on a badge it's because we want to

238

uphold the law and keep people safe, but we have to decide how to interpret and apply the law as we see fit. Just you against all five of them, you might have been laid out on the wrong side of the sod. That you feel bad about what happened shows me you have a strong moral compass, and I admire that. So, my offer still stands."

"Take it, Zeke!" Beecher implored him. "We need you to stand with us!"

"You've brought us this far." Phillips added. "You can't leave the job unfinished!"

Zeke looked at them both in turn. There was no mistaking the sincerity in their faces, and he had to admit Pete Phillips had a point. He couldn't leave these good people in the lurch now, not having started them on this path. Slowly, he nodded.

"When you put it that way, I suppose I could serve as a special deputy for a little while. But only until the sheriff arrives and takes charge of the situation."

"Done!" Mulvenon slapped his desk, then shouted, "Jimmy!"

The deputy opened the door and peeked in. "Yes, sir?"

"Bring three badges out of the strongbox! I've just recruited these good men, and one of them actually has a lawman's experience!"

The deputy did as ordered, and Mulvenon swore them all in and presented them with their badges. "It's getting late, and you probably don't want to start back for Pleasant Grove in the dark. Have you got a room in Prescott for the night?"

Zeke shook his head. "We came straight here when we arrived."

"There's a hotel on the corner; you must have passed it on your way in. It's a bit pricey, but it has a good restaurant. It supplies meals for my prisoners. If you're short on traveling funds, I've got three empty cells in the back you're welcome to bed down in. I'll tell Jimmy to order dinner and breakfast for you, and you can stable your horses for the night just up the street at the livery for a small cost if you tell them I sent you."

"You're too generous, Sheriff, I'm sure I speak for all of us when I gratefully accept your free room and board!" Tom Beecher answered gleefully. "I've never spent the night in jail before, and I have Deputy Zeke to thank for that!"

Zeke laughed. "You're most entirely welcome, Deputy Tom." He felt almost light-hearted now, as if a heavy weight he had carried for way too long had been lifted from his soul.

■ ■ ■ ■

It was past dark after they boarded their mounts at the nearby livery stable and returned to the sheriff's office with their gear to find that their dinner had been delivered while they were gone. Deputy Ciglan had set out cloth-covered plates of thick beef stew and dumplings on his desk in the outer office.

"Sheriff's gone home for the night," he told them. "He says don't leave in the morning until he gets here. I'll show you your cells after you eat."

They stood around the desk and wolfed down their meal, using the large wooden spoons supplied. Zeke eyed the nearby stove and the coffee pot sitting atop it. "That coffee fresh?" he asked Ciglan.

"Fresh this morning, sorry," the deputy replied.

Zeke grimaced. "I suppose for the sake of my stomach, I'll wait for tomorrow's pot."

CHAPTER 31

"Life is sometimes a series of circumstances that are going to happen, even if you didn't envision the same ending from what actually occurs."

Soon after they finished their meal, Deputy Ciglan lit a lantern and led them down a short hallway to the large room that contained six small, boxlike cells. The doors to the three on the right stood open, while the three on the left were closed, locked, and occupied by sleeping prisoners.

"Take your pick," Ciglan told them. "They're all the same, anyways. Guess I don't have to lock you in, but just don't get up and wander around the building in the dark, or I'm liable to shoot you."

Each cell contained a solid wooden platform on the right side, upon which were laid out a thin straw-filled mattress, an even thinner blanket, and a limp pillow. A chamber pot stood in the far left corner opposite the bed, and a small barred window without glass was high up on the wall . . . too high to stand and look out of. There were no solid walls between the cells, only more bars.

"All the comforts of home," Beecher muttered as he entered the first cell. Zeke took the middle cell, and Phillips the last one. When the deputy left, taking the lantern with him, a heavy darkness settled over the room. After a long day on the road, the three men fell asleep almost instantly, despite the thunderous snoring coming from one of the prisoners across the aisle.

Early the next morning, just before sunrise, Deputy Ciglan rolled a serving cart into the room and slid the prisoners' breakfasts on tin plates under their cell doors along with a tin cup of black coffee apiece. Zeke, Beecher, and Phillips were already awake and packing up their gear.

The deputy motioned for them to follow him. "Your grub is out in the office, and there's fresh coffee brewed," he told them as they walked down the hallway. "Sheriff should be here soon to see you on your way."

Beecher and Phillips eagerly dug into the scrambled eggs, fried potatoes, and corn muffins while Zeke drank his first cup of coffee in over a day. As they were eating, the sheriff arrived. "A good morning to you, deputies," he greeted them as he poured himself a cup of coffee. "I neglected to tell you last night to keep your badges out of sight when you return home. We don't want to spook Marshal Seegern and put him on the defensive, or to flight, before I get there. When the time is right you can don them and exert your authority."

He grinned at Zeke and raised his cup. "But I'll wager Deputy Smith had already thought of that."

"I had," Zeke admitted. "I was going to mention it on the ride back, but now it's official."

"How long will it take to find that circuit judge and a bank auditor?" Beecher asked around a mouthful of eggs.

"A day or two, a week at most," Mulvenon replied. "Any longer than that and I'll get word to you. Now I'll wish you all a safe journey home and get back to that mountain of paperwork I have to climb."

Beecher looked at Zeke. "Are you going to eat your breakfast?"

"No. You two can split my share," Zeke answered. "Just save me the corn muffin. I'll eat it later."

"You can have mine, too," Phillips said, handing his muffin to Zeke while Beecher divided up the contents of the third plate and spooned it onto theirs. Zeke slipped both muffins into his coat pocket and poured himself another cup of coffee while the other two ate his portion of food.

The sun was up when they started back to Pleasant Grove. A cool wind came up at their backs, as if to hurry them along, but the pale-blue sky above was devoid of any clouds that might indicate an approaching storm. Their mood was jovial, with Beecher and Phillips discussing the recent turn of events and wishing they could share the news with the absent Jack Hollis.

"We owe him one for telling that shopkeeper about the so-called Apache raid," Beecher said. "He backed us up, and he didn't even know it."

Phillips finally posed the question Zeke had figured would be coming. "One thing I've been curious about, Zeke, ever since you admitted your past occupation. Do you ever miss being a lawman? Seems to me you never really left the job behind. Tom told me a while back that he suspected you were a former peace officer."

Zeke took a moment to work it through. "Let's just say I allowed my fury to get the better of me and, in a red rage, overstepped the boundaries of the law," he answered slowly. "Later, I overstepped my boundaries again with a beautiful young lady who nursed me back to health and showed me how to make up for what I had done." The vision of Manuela de la Rosa flashed across his memory . . . her oval face with high cheekbones, her wide-set brown eyes flecked with green, her upturned nose and smiling mouth, her shining black hair falling in ringlets to her shoulders. "Since then, I've just sort of wandered around helping people who needed it, in any way I could."

Tom Beecher chuckled. "I *knew* there had to be a woman involved! They'll break your heart every time!"

"Actually," Zeke said, "I broke my own heart."

Tom turned sober at that. "I'm not going to make a jest here, my friend, as is my habit. But I do believe that God and the beautiful lady have already forgiven you. You just haven't forgiven yourself yet."

"Paying an endless, self-imposed debt is more a punishment than an obligation," Phillips added. "You're just hurting yourself."

"You may be right," Zeke answered with a touch of sadness. "At least, I'd like to think you are."

Shortly after that exchange, a wagon rounded a sharp curve ahead of them. They moved over and rode single file on their side of the road to allow the wagon to pass by. The driver tipped his hat to them, and they returned the wordless greeting. They continued riding, one behind the other, in silence as they encountered more traffic on the road. Around them, the clusters of houses and side roads slowly thinned out to scattered homes and farm fields until finally they rode through gently rolling terrain of untamed forests and fields. With no more congestion on the road, they could spread out and ride three abreast again. The wind blew unabated, but the temperature warmed up to a tolerable level whenever they rode out of the shadows of trees and through long patches of direct sunlight.

Around midday, Zeke pulled the two corn muffins out of his coat pocket and offered to share them with his companions. They both begged off, claiming they were still full from the extra helping of breakfast they had consumed earlier.

"You're both bad liars," Zeke told them. "But I'm really hungry, so I'll believe you this once." He wolfed down the first muffin and followed it with a long drink from his canteen, then started on the other.

"We should get back to Pleasant Grove just around sunset," Beecher observed. "I suppose I can wait to eat until after I get home."

"I've been thinking about when we get back," Phillips said. "Who can we tell about our new appointments if we have to be secretive about it?"

Zeke thought for a moment as he chewed a mouthful of muffin. "We should be able to tell the Schneiders and Stu Jenkins, since they're involved in this. It's up to you to decide whether or not you want to worry them, but your wives will have to know, and I'll tell the Stevens family. But that's all."

"I agree," Beecher replied.

"I can ride on to the Jenkins place and tell Stu before I head home," Phillips offered. "Then all we have to do is wait for the sheriff to show up."

"Hopefully sooner rather than later. You've waited long enough for justice to be done." Even as Zeke said it, he couldn't suppress a nagging worry that had grown on him as they drew closer to Pleasant Grove. They'd succeeded in their task so far, but there was plenty that could still go wrong.

CHAPTER 32

"Justice delayed is still justice served when the guilty are made to pay for their crimes."

They rode into town just before sunset and found Ludwig and Jacob Schneider in the process of closing the mercantile for the day. Since the sidewalks were practically deserted just then, they stopped, helped them carry display goods in from the sidewalk, and told them quickly about the results of the trip to Prescott. A three-quarter moon had just risen above the trees when they reached Tom Beecher's home an hour later and bade him goodnight. The moon provided more than enough light for Zeke and Pete Phillips to follow the road without much difficulty. Further on, Zeke stopped and dismounted at the gate to the Stevens home. Phillips said goodbye and rode on toward Stu Jenkins's place to tell him what had happened, before returning to his own

249

homestead.

Zeke entered and closed the gate behind him. A single lit lantern on the corner of the porch, and the lamplight from inside the house shining through the windows, were like beacons in the darkness guiding him home.

He rode up to the cabin and called out, "Hello the house! It's Zeke out here, and I'm back for my promised cake!"

The front door inched open a crack, and Nana peeked out, then threw the door wide open. Willie rushed out past her onto the porch, bounded down the steps as Zeke dismounted, and hugged him warmly. "We were worried about you!" Willie exclaimed.

Through the open door, Zeke could see Rebecca standing at the kitchen table holding a plate covered with a cloth. "We kept your supper warm," she called out to him. "Come in and eat before it gets cold."

"Let me put Mule up for the night first," Zeke called back. "Then I'll be right in!"

Willie moved to the end of the porch and picked up the lantern. "I'll help you."

Later, at the table as he ate, with the others hanging on his every word, Zeke related all the details of their trip, the meeting with the county sheriff, and their night in jail. Nana got up from her chair and refilled

Zeke's coffee cup twice as he spoke. When he finished his story, and his meal, Willie exclaimed, "You're really a deputy sheriff? Can I see your badge?"

Zeke dug around in his coat pocket and produced the shiny metal star, placing it on the table for all to see and marvel at. "I suppose now, Miss Nana, I'll have to let you dye my coat black so I have something presentable to pin this on when I'm allowed to," he joked.

"It's about time," she said. "I was beginning to think you were too stubborn to ever come around to my way of thinking! Ready for your cake now?"

"Yes, ma'am! Been thinking about it all day long!" he replied, rubbing his hands together.

The next morning it was business as usual around the Stevens homestead. Zeke awoke refreshed, the floor of the empty stall being infinitely more familiar and comfortable than the jail bed he had occupied. He dressed and began his chores of feeding the animals and cleaning out their stalls by the light of a lamp. Outside, he could hear Willie chopping firewood, and Nana was collecting the day's eggs while Rebecca busily prepared the morning meal. Everything felt so normal as the sun rose to start the new day that it was easy to forget a local storm of their own making was brewing.

At breakfast, Rebecca suggested they should go out to the apple orchard soon to trim the dead branches and clear any dead trees and underbrush, in preparation for the next growing season. There was also the need to replenish their wood supply.

"If you're planning to drive the wagon down that path through the woods to the pond, there's a downed tree across it that'll have to be cleared first," Zeke said. "Willie and I should go out there today and take care of that. We'll also make sure the passageway is wide enough for the wagon to pass through. It's pretty narrow now."

Rebecca nodded. "At one time it was a wide enough road. But I imagine it has become pretty overgrown."

"You can take the rest of that cake I baked for you to munch on while you work," Nana said. "If you leave it here, Rebecca and I will just wind up finishing it off, and we have to be mindful of our girlish figures."

Rebecca smiled at that. "You can leave us just one piece each, if it wouldn't trouble you too much."

Zeke winked at Willie. "We won't starve if I do."

After Willie's morning lessons, he and Zeke went to the barn, picking up the axe at the woodpile on their way. They put the axe, a canteen of water, two bow saws, a hatchet, and the remaining cake wrapped in a cloth into the wheelbarrow Zeke had rinsed out. When they arrived at the fallen tree, it was lower to the ground than before because many of the branches holding it up had finally cracked and broken under the weight of the thick trunk. They set to work chopping and sawing off the larger branches that still pointed skyward, dragging them to the side of the pathway, and piling them up. Zeke took the axe and began to chop at the trunk where it had split from the stump but was still attached by strips of torn bark. The trunk was dried out, but not yet rotten, so once he separated it from the stump it was light enough for them to drag out of the way. With some effort, they slid and rolled it over so the branches that had held it off the ground were now on top.

"I'll clear these remaining branches off and start chopping the trunk into manage-able sections," Zeke told Willie. "You take the hatchet and move on toward the pond, chopping down any saplings and bushes that have grown up. You should be able to make out the original edges of the road as

253

you go. When you finish that task, we'll rest and have some cake."

When Willie returned, close to an hour later, Zeke had chopped and stacked up at least half of the dead tree. As they sat and ate the cake, passing the canteen between them to wash it down with, Zeke kept opening and closing his right hand and wiggling his fingers.

"Something wrong?" Willie asked.

"Not really," Zeke replied. "Just my hand sometimes feels a little colder than the rest of me lately, and it's a bit stiff right now from gripping the axe handle. Old age must be catching up to me."

"Nana gets that all the time; her hands and feet are always cold," Willie observed.

"She's led a hard life and has been knocked around quite a bit by it, but she has a warm heart, and that's what counts." Zeke kept making a fist and then extending his fingers. "I just wish this wasn't my gun hand."

"You've been knocked around quite a bit, too," Willie said.

"Don't I know it and feel it!" Zeke grunted as he stood up. "We'd best get back to work now, or this job will never get finished. Remember, Willie, to always try to finish what you start, no matter how daunting the task or how punishing on mind and body it may be."

"I'll remember," Willie promised.

In another hour Willie had chopped and sawed the road clear of any obstructions to the beginning of the woods, and Zeke had finished cutting the fallen tree into pieces. They loaded the wheelbarrow with all the cut wood Zeke could manage to push, and Willie carried one piece on his shoulder, as they walked back to the house and wood-pile. Once unloaded, they returned to the work site to load up the tools in the wheel-barrow, then returned them to the barn.

"We can pick up the rest of what I cut with the wheelbarrow or the wagon tomor-row, now that the road is wide enough to drive on," Zeke said as they stood at the well rinsing themselves off. When Willie looked back at the tree line and marveled at how much wider and passable the over-grown path of the morning was, he felt a sense of pride in their shared accomplish-ment.

Nana was resting in her rocking chair on the porch and called out to them as they approached the house. "With all the chop-ping and sawing I heard out there today, I thought you were taking down all the trees in the forest!"

"With Willie's help, I don't doubt we could have!" Zeke answered with a chuckle as he slapped the boy on the back.

CHAPTER 33

"Meeting violence with violence is sometimes the only language an aggressor can, or will, understand. It is a necessary evil."

After breakfast the following morning, Willie and Zeke went out with the wheelbarrow to pick up the rest of the chopped wood from the road they had cleared the previous day. On their way back with their load, Zeke suddenly halted and dropped the wheelbarrow handles as they exited the trees. Willie, a chunk of wood on his shoulder, bumped into him from behind. Just visible past the barn, a familiar hulking figure of a man was mounting the porch steps. Out in the corral, Mule and Molly began to skitter around frantically, calling out to unseen horses whose scent they must have caught on the morning breeze.

Zeke drew his pistol. "Run to the corral!" he whispered to Willie. "Stay low and keep the barn between you and the house so you can't be seen from the yard! Get inside and get up to the hayloft for your rifle! Do you remember how I taught you to load it?"

Willie's voice trembled as he replied, "Yes, sir!"

"I'll go around by the chicken coop. Go!" Zeke commanded, and they started to run.

Zeke soon outdistanced Willie and swiftly reached the chicken coop. He peeked around it and saw to his dismay that Big Otto hadn't come alone. Deputy Spinks, pistol drawn, stood peering in the front door of the barn, while a mounted Marshal Seegern watched him. A chill ran up Zeke's spine. Had Willie already gone in through the back? If not, Spinks would likely shoot the boy the second he spotted him.

There was no other choice. Zeke stepped out from beside the chicken coop and into view. Immediately, Spinks and Seegern trained their pistols on him.

"Drop your gun!" the marshal ordered.

Rebecca and Nana were washing the morning dishes when the front door flew open and slammed against the wall. In the doorway stood Deputy Otto Manholtz.

"Where's your hired hand?" he demanded, ducking his head as he stepped inside.

Rebecca dropped her dishrag and rushed over to confront the intruder; hands clenched into fists at her sides. "You get out of my house!" she hissed at him.

Nana moved quickly to join her, catching a glimpse past Otto of Marshal Seegern in the yard astride his horse.

Otto sneered at their effort to bar his way. "Maybe he's hiding in that back room, or up in the loft?"

He pushed past them, then halted at a triumphant yell from Deputy Spinks outside: "We've got him!"

Zeke raised his hands. As Spinks approached, the marshal said, "I want to have a talk with you about the little trip you took the other day, where you went and who you spoke to."

Zeke showed no sign of the surprise he felt. Briefly, he recalled Sheila Bacron outside her boardinghouse, watching them in the early morning as she swept her porch and the walkway clean, and guessed who Seegern's source of information was. If he were a cursing man, he'd have done it right then. Instead, he said, "What business is it of yours?" as he walked slowly forward. Spinks halted and began to back up, his pistol still pointed at Zeke's midsection.

"Everything that goes on in *my* town is *my* business," Seegern answered dryly. "Nobody comes into, or goes out of, *my* town that I don't know the reason for it. If you won't tell me what I want to know, one of the others will when we pick them up. When they see you're in custody, they shouldn't give us any trouble."

An evil leer spread over Otto's face, and he grabbed Rebecca's chin in his beefy hand. "When I finish with your hired man, maybe I'll come back so we can get to know each other better!"

"You get out of here, you . . ." Nana began to snarl at him.

He slapped her hard enough to send her staggering back against the table. "Not a word out of you, old hag!" he bellowed, then turned to leave. He stepped out onto the porch, stopping at the top of the steps. "Let me have him for a few minutes!" he called out, pounding a fist into his palm.

Spinks looked at the marshal. Seegern nodded. Spinks stepped up to Zeke and jammed the barrel of his pistol into Zeke's stomach. "Get over there!" he growled.

A sudden loud boom cchoed inside the house. The next second, Otto's chest exploded in a shower of blood and tatters of torn shirt and flesh. As the cloud of gun smoke that swirled around him drifted away on the breeze, he staggered forward and pitched headlong down the stairs to the ground.

Through the open doorway, Zeke saw Nana, a shocked look on her face, both barrels of the shotgun they kept behind the door still smoking in her hands. Spinks and Seegern were motionless, gaping at Otto's corpse as if unable to believe what had just happened.

Zeke grabbed Spinks's wrist and twisted the deputy's gun down and away from his belly. It fired harmlessly into the ground beside them. He punched Spinks in the face with his free hand, just as the marshal raised his pistol and pointed it at Zeke.

A rifle shot cracked from the barn. The marshal ducked as Willie stepped outside, weapon still pointed at Seegern. Before Willie could cock the rifle and get off another shot, the marshal wheeled his horse around and galloped out through the open front gate.

Zeke hit Spinks in the face again. The deputy crumpled to the ground, dropping his pistol, his broken nose gushing blood. As he rolled over and tried to crawl away, Zeke leapt on him, pulling Spinks's own knife from the beaded leather scabbard the deputy wore on his gun belt. Sitting on his back, Zeke grabbed a handful of the man's hair and pulled his head up, placing the knife edge at the deputy's hairline. He pushed the blade so strongly it drew blood.

"Now tell me what happened at the Bidwell place!" he growled, "or I'm going to scalp you right now! You're an old Indian fighter, Spinks, you must know a man can be scalped and still live a good long life! Of course, nobody ever wants to look at him, and he has to wear a hat for the rest of his days indoors and out, but he's alive. Maybe you can add your own hair to your collection!"

"All right, all right!" Spinks screamed. "We rode out to the Bidwell place that morning, and Otto strangled the both of them! I shot arrows into the bodies and left the necklace on the ground nearby so people would think the Apaches had done it."

"The necklace is one you took off some poor Apache girl?"

"Yes." Spinks spat blood from his mouth. "We fired the house, too, so the smoke would bring the neighbors. Then we headed back through the woods, cutting over to pick up the road so we could ride toward the scene like we were just coming up on it."

"Whose notion was it to stage the raid? Why'd you all do it?" Zeke asked, though he'd already figured out the truth.

"The marshal's," Spinks said. "The whole idea was to gain control of the Bidwells' land and get rid of Will Stevens in the process! That coward Seegern is a great schemer, all right. When we got off by ourselves and were crossing a clearing, he sent Jack Hollis off on a fool's errand. Stevens stopped to look for tracks, and the marshal turned around and shot him — or tried to. Only he's not much good at it, so his first shot killed Stevens's horse instead. His second shot did the trick when Stevens jumped clear of the falling animal. The marshal told us to fire our rifles several times, like we were going after the raiders, and hide in the woods on the far side of the clearing. When the others arrived, we were supposed to shoot some more and then come out, saying we ran the Apaches off."

Rebecca had reached them, rifle in hand, in time to hear Spinks's confession. Anger flashed across her face, then shock as Willie stepped forward and pointed his rifle at the deputy. "Willie, don't!" she cried out to her son.

Willie heard his mother, but he didn't lower his rifle. A wave of hatred washed over him at this sniveling coward who had helped kill the father Willie loved. His stomach fluttered, and he was so tense and angry that his limbs trembled. He felt light-headed as he stood there, face flushed and burning hot, his finger tight against the trigger, and he feared he might collapse in a heap before exacting revenge for himself and his family.

"Listen to your mother, son," Zeke said quietly.

Willie's heart pounded in his chest, and hot tears rolled down his cheeks. "He helped kill my father! He deserves to die for it!"

"Look at Otto, Willie, look at him! That man is dead!" Zeke's voice was urgent now. "Do you want to shoot this man dead? I won't blame you if you do, and I won't try to stop you. But just know he'll haunt your dreams for the rest of your life. If you pull that trigger, you'll see his face every time you close your eyes . . . his face as you see it now and as it looks after you've killed him. You'll never be rid of him!"

Willie stood rigid as Zeke's words took hold. There wasn't a sound in the yard, except for his own harsh breathing and Spinks's occasional snuffling gulps. Willie stared at the terrified deputy and thought about seeing that face in his mind for years, maybe forever. That face, shattered by a bullet he fired.

His rage subsided, and he slowly lowered the rifle.

"Good boy!" Zeke said softly. "Get some rope from the barn so we can tie him up, and then go catch his horse for me — there's no time to saddle Mule."

After they had secured Spinks, Zeke retrieved his and the deputy's pistols from the ground. He holstered his own and stuffed the other under his gun belt. "If he gives you any trouble, shoot him in the leg," he told the Stevens family as he mounted Spinks's horse. "We'll need his testimony later."

He urged the horse to a gallop and raced out the front gate and down the road toward town after the marshal.

A few miles down the road, by the Beecher farm, he saw Tom just mounting his own horse, rifle in hand. Zeke reined up. "Now would be a good time to pin on that badge!" he shouted. "Big Otto is dead, Spinks is tied up at the Stevens place, and Marshal Seegern is on the run!"

"I heard the shots and saw him race by!"

Beecher replied as he came out onto the road. "Should I go get Pete Phillips?"

"No time. We've got to go after Seegern *now.*"

Tom nodded, a fierce grin on his face. "The sheriff is going to be real upset that we didn't keep the peace until he got here!"

"Let the sheriff find his own fight!" Zeke said as they set off at a gallop. "This one is ours!"

CHAPTER 34

"When the storm is over, and the world feels so fresh and clean, it is hard to remember the fear and anguish you felt during the maelstrom."

Zeke and Tom reined in briefly at the top of the rise overlooking Pleasant Grove. All seemed quiet down below, but the streets appeared eerily deserted for the time of day.

"Do you think he's still down there?" Tom asked breathlessly.

"Probably holed up in the jail," Zeke replied as he withdrew the deputy sheriff badge from his vest pocket and carefully pinned it on over his heart. "His type doesn't let go of power easily. We'll have to root him out!"

He pulled the rifle out of Spinks's saddle scabbard and checked it for load and lever action. "We should go in slow, so as to not raise any alarm, and head for the mercantile.

That'll give us a good view of the jail across the street. We can warn anybody we might meet along the way to get under cover, although . . ." He peered at the town spread out below them. "It looks like they already have. If any shooting starts, get inside the mercantile as fast as you can, and we'll adjust our strategy from there."

"Sure wish Phillips was here with us," Beecher said. "He's a crack shot."

"We'll make do," Zeke replied grimly. "Let's go."

They rode slowly into town, single file, with Zeke in the lead. Horses were tied to hitching posts, and wagons were parked on either side of the street, their owners noticeably absent from the thoroughfare. As they passed the deserted sidewalks, Zeke felt the curious gazes of onlookers peeking out at them from windows and doorways.

"Don't tie up in front of the mercantile," he said over his shoulder as they neared their destination. "We may need a clear field of fire, and there's already a freight wagon partially in the way."

As they rode past the mercantile, rifles at the ready and fingers on the triggers, Zeke spotted Jacob and Ludwig inside, looking out on either side of the front window. He nodded to them, while Tom kept a wary eye on the bank across the street. They dismounted in front of the feed and grain store and tied their horses securely to the hitching post there.

"What's Seegern up to?" Beecher whispered as they walked back the short distance to the mercantile. "He should have been blasting away at us by now! Do you think he left town already?"

"We'll find out soon," Zeke answered. Their footsteps on the sidewalk seemed unusually loud in the silence that hung over the street. The freight wagon in front of the mercantile was partly unloaded, and they had to move around barrels and wooden boxes piled up on the walkway to reach the front door. The elder Schneider ushered them in and quickly closed the door behind them.

"What is happening, Zeke?" he demanded. "The marshal and his deputies ride out of town this morning, and then only he returns, riding like all the hounds of Hell are chasing him! He doesn't even tie up his horse but leaps off and runs into the bank. Next we hear shots! There were tellers and customers in there, and nobody's come out since!"

"Calm down, Papa," Jacob said soothingly. "Zeke is here now, and all will be well."

"Otto is dead, and Spinks is a prisoner out at the Stevens home," Zeke answered as he peered carefully out the front window. "Seegern's got hostages now. He'll want to trade them for his safe escape, that's why he's not shooting. Is there a back door into the bank or the jail?"

Jacob shook his head. "Only a side door into the alley between the jail and the saloon. I've been watching it from here, and nobody has gone in or come out."

"Well then," Zeke said as he handed his rifle to Beecher, "I best go over and hear his terms."

He stepped out of the mercantile and moved to the front edge of the sidewalk, arms stretched out at his sides, palms facing forward. "Seegern!" he called out toward the bank. "Let's talk this over before anyone else gets killed!"

The front door of the bank opened a crack. "Come ahead!" came the marshal's reply.

Despite Zeke's brave words to Tom and the Schneiders, he wasn't certain Seegern wouldn't just gun him down, but he stepped off the sidewalk and walked slowly across the street toward the bank anyway, his arms still outstretched. As he drew close, he spied a shotgun barrel poking out of the slightly open door.

"That's close enough! Stop there!" the marshal barked. Zeke halted in mid-stride at the edge of the street just in front of the sidewalk. "Let's hear what you have to say!"

Zeke drew a long breath. "I know you're holding people in there with you. I was wondering if you might want to trade their freedom for Deputy Spinks and any future testimony he might give against you."

"Spinks?"

"That's right. The deputy you ran out on and left to his fate. He's a little the worse for wear, but he's alive and under guard, out at the Stevens place. I'll send someone to bring him here, and you can have him if you let those people go unharmed."

"I see you're wearing a badge now," Seegern snarled. "That what your little trip heading toward Prescott was about? Somebody gave you some authority here?"

"That's right," Zeke said.

Seegern snickered. "Well then, here's my thought. These people come out, and *both* you and Spinks come in. And I want fresh horses tied up outside here. We all leave town together, and Spinks and I let you go when we're far enough away. I'm sure there will be no tricks or close pursuit."

"It will take some time to get Spinks

here," Zeke said. "I don't plan to stand out here all day, so suppose I go over and sit in front of the mercantile where you can see me and know that I'm not plotting anything."

"We have a deal," Seegern said and closed the door without another word.

Zeke turned around and walked back across the street. Tom Beecher and Jacob Schneider, both holding rifles pointed at the bank, stepped out the mercantile door and met him on the sidewalk. "Well?" Tom asked.

"He'll trade his hostages for me, Spinks, and fresh horses," Zeke said. "Says he'll let me go when they've made good their escape."

"You know that won't happen," Jacob said. "You'll get a bullet in the back a mile outside of town!"

"I know. But it's our best chance of getting those people out of there unharmed. Does your father remember how many were in the bank when Seegern showed up?"

Jacob gnawed his lip. "No more than five, I think he said."

"Then here's the plan." Zeke pulled a wooden box from the sidewalk behind the freight wagon, slid it along the walkway, and sat down on it in sight of the bank. "Tom, you ride out to the Stevens place with Spinks's horse and bring the deputy back here. Drop him off with me, then ride back out like you're leaving to get the horses Seegern wants. Tie up at the end of the street, out of sight, and sneak back on foot to the alley door Jacob told us about. Seegern won't be able to see you coming unless he steps out the front door of the bank, and he won't do that. When the hostages are safely clear, Spinks and I will go inside. Jacob will signal you from here when that happens. You wait a minute, then make a big ruckus at the alley door just as loud as you can. I have to stay where Seegern can see me until you return so he doesn't think I'm up to something."

Beecher looked worried. "Do you really think this will work?"

Zeke shrugged. "If it doesn't, at least they won't have any hostages in there, and you can blast them out. He and Spinks will have seen to it that I'll be beyond caring at that point."

Beecher nodded grimly and walked away toward the feed and grain store where they'd tied their mounts. As he rode by a couple of minutes later, leading Spinks's horse behind him, he looked down at Zeke.

"Good luck, my friend. May God protect you."

"I sure do hope He does." Zeke watched him go, then turned to Jacob Schneider. "Jacob, is there any coffee in there on the stove? I sure could use a cup right about now."

"I'll bring you some." Jacob ducked into the mercantile, returning shortly with a steaming ceramic mugful. As he handed it to Zeke, he said, "I admire you, Zeke Smith, for being willing to possibly trade your life for the lives of five others you don't even know."

"I can't see any other choice," Zeke said with resignation as he cradled the warm mug in both hands. "I hope it won't turn out badly for any of us. You'd best get back inside now and keep your father calm. I shouldn't be seen talking to anybody too much, or Seegern will think I'm hatching a plot against him."

Two hours crawled by. A few curious on-lookers ventured out of the buildings where they'd taken shelter, only to have a quick look around and return indoors before any trouble started. From time to time, Zeke idly spun the cylinder of Spinks's pistol. Finally, far down the road, he spied two horsemen slowly approaching. As they drew closer, he saw it was Tom Beecher, leading Spinks's horse with the forlorn deputy precariously balanced in the saddle. Spinks's forehead was bandaged where Zeke had unintentionally cut him by pushing the knife too hard, his nose and eyes were swollen, and his hands were still tied behind him.

Zeke stood up and stepped into the street to meet them.

CHAPTER 35

"Always stand up for a just cause, even if you stand alone. Others will join you when they come to understand the truth you already know."

Tom Beecher reined up and stopped as Zeke stepped forward to help Spinks dismount. The deputy slid from his horse and just stood there, head down and eyes shut as if in pain. He and his horse were between Zeke and the bank, briefly shielding Zeke from view. Swiftly, Zeke slipped his pistol out of its holster and stuck it into the back of his gun belt, then replaced it with Spinks's pistol.

"The Stevens clan is on their way here," Tom said. "They were on the road in their wagon, just past my place, bringing Spinks in when I met them. They wouldn't turn around and go home, so I outdistanced them coming back here. Nana Stevens tied that dirty rag around his cut forehead and reset his broken nose for him. I guess she was none too gentle about it; he was still crying when I put him on his horse."

Mention of the Stevens family reminded Zeke of just what Marshal Seegern and his thugs had done to them, and he fought down a surge of fury.

"Tie up the horse in front of the bank, and go fetch two more," Zeke said for Spinks to hear. He took the deputy's arm and led him out into the open street. As they approached the bank, Tom eased by them. Zeke watched him dismount at the hitching rail, tie up the riderless horse, remount his own, and ride slowly back up the street.

They halted in front of the bank, several feet from the wooden walkway. "Here he is, Seegern, alive and somewhat well, as promised," Zeke shouted. "You get us inside when the others come out!"

The front door opened a crack. "Drop your gun first and untie him!" Seegern ordered.

Zeke stepped back so he was slightly behind Spinks, then carefully removed the pistol from his holster, leaned forward, and slipped it into Spinks's empty one.

"Fair enough?" he asked.

Not waiting for an answer, he turned the deputy sideways and untied his hands in plain view of the marshal. A full minute passed with no word or activity from inside. From the corner of his eye, Zeke watched Tom Beecher edging slowly down the sidewalk. Tom reached the alley between the bank building and the saloon and ducked into it out of sight. Spinks grunted, and for a bad moment Zeke wondered if the deputy had noticed Tom but then dismissed the thought. With his eyes swollen and watering, Spinks couldn't see much of anything more than a few feet in front of him.

The bank door flew open. Three men and two women, one of them very young and very pregnant, rushed out. Zeke had a flash of memory of another pregnant woman long ago in a dusty Texas town, as he waved them off toward Doc Carne's office. "Get down the street and away from here!"

"He's robbed the bank!" one of the men cried out as he ran down the sidewalk.

Marshal Seegern stepped into the open doorway, a short-barreled shotgun cradled in his arm and leveled at Zeke and Spinks. He held a carpetbag in his other hand.

"Come on in, boys," Seegern snarled at them. "No sudden moves, or I'll shoot you both. Where are the other horses?"

"They're being brought up now," Zeke answered as he and Spinks moved forward.

"He sent the other fellow to get them," Spinks said. He caught his foot on the edge of the sidewalk, and Zeke grabbed his arm to keep him from falling.

They entered the gloomy interior of the bank, the heavy fabric curtains still drawn across the front window. It took a few seconds for their eyes to adjust after Zeke pushed the door closed behind them. Directly ahead of them, behind Seegern, were the teller windows. To the right was the marshal's office and the jail, separated from the bank lobby by a wall of wrought iron bars.

Looking past the marshal, Zeke saw that the door to the tall safe behind the teller counter stood wide open. He stepped around behind Spinks and backed up, hands raised, moving toward the left so Seegern would move to the right. The marshal ended up facing Zeke, with his back to the jail and the door that led out to the alley.

"Now what?" Zeke asked.

"Now we wait for the horses to arrive so I can get out of here once and for all!" Seegern growled.

"Then the town can get some *real* law

enforcement instead of a thug and his bullies with their hands in the till?" Zeke asked, his voice cold with anger.

"Mighty brave talk from a man who could be shot to pieces before the day is out!" the marshal replied with equal fervor. "In fact —"

A loud banging on the alleyway door cut him off, accompanied by shouting and a gunshot. Startled, Seegern instinctively turned to see what was happening behind him, swinging the shotgun away from Zeke and Spinks. Zeke yanked the pistol from the back of his gun belt and crouched down as he pointed it at the distracted marshal.

"Dave, watch out! He's got a gun!" Spinks shouted, a heartbeat too late as Zeke fired.

The bullet struck Seegern in the upper left arm and exited out his back, shattering the shoulder blade. The impact of the shot made the marshal stagger back a step and drop the carpetbag. He triggered the shotgun by reflex, firing both barrels into the teller counter, which exploded in a spray of wood splinters and pulverized glass. Then Seegern dropped to the floor.

As Zeke stepped forward to relieve Seegern of his weapons, Spinks drew his own pistol, pointed it at Zeke, and pulled the trigger. There was an audible click, then another as he thumbed the hammer back and tried again with the same result.

Zeke snorted. "You didn't think I'd be stupid enough to give you a loaded gun, did you?"

He stepped up to Spinks and swung his pistol against the side of the man's head, knocking him unconscious. He snatched the empty gun from Spinks's hand as the deputy fell.

The front door of the bank flew open, and Tom Beecher rushed inside, followed by Jacob Schneider, their rifles leveled and ready to shoot. They saw Zeke standing there, pistols in his hands, and two men on the floor at his feet, neither one moving, a thin fog of gun smoke hanging in the air.

Jacob surveyed the room. "Is it over?"

"It's over," Zeke replied. "Go get two cells ready for them."

"Spinks isn't dead?" Beecher stepped forward and nudged the deputy's body with his foot.

"No, just knocked out when I buffaloed him," Zeke replied. "Better send for the doctor, though. Seegern's shot and bleeding."

"Doc Carne is just outside," Jacob told him. "We brought him along with us."

As Tom and Jacob dragged the unconscious Spinks into the jail and searched for the cell keys, Seegern groaned and struggled to his knees, clutching his limp left arm. Zeke bent and hauled the man to his feet, then jammed his cocked pistol up under the marshal's chin.

"I should blow the top of your head off for what you've done to the people of this town!" he snarled as fresh rage welled up inside him.

"You won't find the redemption you seek if you do, Deputy Smith." Sheriff Mulvenon's voice carried from the open bank doorway.

Zeke looked at the sheriff, saw Doc Carne beside him, then spied Rebecca, Nana, and Willie standing in the street behind them along with Ludwig Schneider and a crowd of townspeople.

"I just got here, earlier than you might have expected me to, with a deputy, the circuit court judge, and the bank auditor," Mulvenon said. "These good people behind me told me what happened here today. It's time for the law — not you — to bring Marshal Seegern what he deserves."

Zeke pushed his pistol a little harder underneath Seegern's chin, his eyes cold. "All right then, I'll settle accounts with you for twenty dollars!"

"Twenty dollars?" Seegern gasped.

"Twenty dollars," Zeke barked. "I have to hire some fellows with a wagon to go out to the Stevens place and retrieve Otto's carcass and bury it somewhere before he starts to stink!"

Seegern glanced down at the carpetbag on the floor, then pushed it forward with his foot.

"Not *that* money, you thief," Zeke snapped. "It belongs to the townspeople! Twenty dollars out of your own pocket!"

Eyes wide with fear, Seegern shoved his uninjured right hand into his pants pocket, withdrew a handful of coins, and held them out. Zeke plucked a twenty-dollar gold piece from the man's palm, then holstered his pistol and stepped back. "He's all yours now, Doc."

CHAPTER 36

"Happy endings are many times tinged with sadness and loss but should still be held dear in your heart."

The jail and bank became a beehive of activity in the following days. The tellers returned to clean up the mess, count the money from the former marshal's carpetbag and lock it back in the safe, while the auditor pored over the bank's books and records. Sheriff Mulvenon and the circuit court judge, Oliver Brooks, busily set up a public court of inquiry in the jail, having as many chairs brought in to seat witnesses and onlookers as would fit in the room. Special deputies Zeke Smith, Tom Beecher, and Pete Phillips took turns guarding the prisoners, along with Deputy Mike Walken, who had accompanied the sheriff to Pleasant Grove.

Within a week Judge Brooks convened his inquest. The jail was crowded with an overflow audience of local men and women as the proceedings began, with the accused men sitting silently in their cells listening to it all. The first item on the agenda was the deaths of the Bidwells and Will Stevens during the alleged Apache raid. Tom Beecher, Stu Jenkins, and Pete Phillips testified as to what they saw and did that day, and former deputy Joe Spinks was brought out of his cell to tell his damning story, which caused gasps of anguish and tears from many in the audience. Sheriff Mulvenon produced the Apache ceremonial necklace left behind at the scene and explained its significance. He also testified that Marshal Seegern had failed to provide any detailed report of the incident. Seegern himself steadfastly refused to testify, and the proceedings were adjourned for the day.

The jail was just as packed the next day, and Judge Brooks allowed additional testimony that spoke to what he called "abuse of power," even though the inquiry was only intended to determine the how and why of the untimely deaths. Beecher and several others testified that Seegern and his deputies pressured them into making improvements on their properties that only seemed to hasten bank foreclosures in many cases.

Ludwig Schneider, along with a few other merchants, described being forced to rent bank-owned properties they didn't want or need to conduct their business. Zeke told the story of the nighttime raid on the Stevens home, after which Doc Carne and Tom Beecher attested to the freight driver's confession about how he came to participate in the shooting.

Their testimony was followed by a preliminary report from the bank auditor, Charles Picard, citing many irregularities in bank records and assets that indicated some larger accounts were being raided of funds, foreclosures were overvalued at the time of resale, and total tax collections were under-reported.

At the end of the day, Judge Brooks found probable cause existed to bind Seegern and Spinks over for trial at the county seat on charges of murder, attempted murder, extortion, bank fraud, and aiding and abetting in the commission of a crime.

A day later, a caravan left town behind a freight wagon, whose drivers had spent the entire siege of the bank in the saloon drinking and staying out of the line of fire. Afterward, Zeke hired them to pick up Otto's corpse at the Stevens property and dispose of it under the watchful eyes of Nana and Rebecca. The sheriff then pressed them into unpaid service transporting the shackled prisoners when it came time for his own departure.

Prior to leaving, the sheriff called Zeke, Tom, and Pete into the jail and thanked them for their service to the county and the territory. "Keep your badges, men," he told them. "I may need to call on you again sometime. You did a fine job here in Pleasant Grove. In fact, I'd say you're invaluable to me since I still can't offer you any pay."

Jacob Schneider was there also, having volunteered to watch over the jail and provide security for the bank until the town elected a new marshal. The sheriff appointed him interim marshal and pinned Seegern's old badge on him. Zeke and the others, all smiles, watched the impromptu ceremony and congratulated him. Afterwards, the sheriff and his deputy on horseback, and the judge and auditor in a buggy, followed the prisoners' wagon as it lumbered and rattled down the street past a crowd gathered to watch and cheer as they would a parade.

The three special deputies said their goodbyes out on the street, after the sheriff and his group had left, with hearty handshakes, good-natured laughter, and slaps on the back. Tom and Pete had their horses saddled and ready, and Zeke waited for the Stevens wagon to pick him up.

When the others had headed home, Zeke walked over to the mercantile to wait for his transport. He marveled at how giddy the mood around town was. People went about their daily business as if an oppressive weight had been lifted from their shoulders. Everyone smiled and waved to him and to each other as they passed by. Out in front of the mercantile, Spinks's horse was tied to the hitching rail with a hand-lettered sign pinned to the saddle that read *This Horse and Rig For Sale. See John Turner, Blacksmith.* Zeke hefted the rifle he still carried and thought about returning it to the empty saddle scabbard but decided Willie might like to have it instead. He entered the mercantile and was warmly greeted by Ludwig Schneider, who came around from behind the counter to shake his hand.

"I just wanted to say goodbye," Zeke said.

Schneider raised an eyebrow. "That sounds so final, my dear friend. Are you going away?"

"Perhaps," Zeke replied with a twinge of sadness. "I haven't decided yet. I want to thank you for directing me out to the

Stevens place so many months ago. I think you helped save my life."

Schneider smiled. "It was my pleasure to do so."

The rattle of wheels and a horse's whinny told Zeke the Stevens wagon had pulled up out front. Zeke squeezed the old man's shoulder and went outside. Rebecca was at the reins, Nana on the seat beside her. Zeke joined Willie in the back of the wagon, and they started off.

As the wagon topped the rise above the town, Zeke stared back at the sunny streets of Pleasant Grove. The sadness he'd felt in the mercantile grew on him as he realized what he needed to do.

"I've been thinking," he said. "Once we've finished getting the orchard ready for the next growing season, I might move on."

Rebecca pulled back on the reins, bringing the wagon to a halt. "What are you talking about, Zeke?" she demanded, turning around in her seat. "This is your home! You can't just pack up and leave us!"

Nana patted Rebecca's arm. "Our place was just one of his homes while the purpose that brought him to us was being served. I saw that early on."

Willie broke his stunned silence, tears

welling up in his eyes. "But where will you go?"

"I don't know," Zeke answered. "Maybe I'll drift back toward Texas and look up some old friends there. Mule and I are getting too old to tolerate the cold and damp very well when the seasons around these parts change anyway."

Rebecca stirred up Molly, and the wagon eased forward again. They rode along in silence for a long time while a sunny spring day unfolded around them, promising warmth and renewal with each passing mile. When they finally reached home, Zeke jumped down from the wagon and opened the front gate to the farmstead. As if sensing his presence, Mule began to bray loudly from the corral behind the barn.

"Yes, old girl!" Zeke called out as he closed the gate after the wagon passed through. "I'm finally back again!"

With the wagon stopped in front of the house and everyone out, Zeke turned to Willie and handed him the rifle he'd carried all the way from town. "You should have this now," he said. "I believe you've earned it."

Willie glanced at Rebecca, and she smiled, nodding. As they mounted the porch steps, Nana scuffed her foot on the bottom one.

"We scrubbed and scrubbed, but those bloodstains are still there where that pig Otto bled on it!" She sighed. "At least that monster will never threaten anyone ever again!"

"It will wear off," Zeke told her. "Everything changes with time and exposure to the weather."

The next day, Zeke and Willie drove the wagon out to the orchard and started clearing brush and dead branches, a task that took them three whole days to complete.

After dinner on the third evening, Zeke hugged and kissed Nana and Rebecca as he bid them goodnight, something he had never done before. Last of all, he hugged Willie close and whispered to him, "Grow up tall and straight, Willie my son. Be a good man."

They all knew he would not be there in the morning.

EPILOGUE

From the journal of William "Willie" Stevens

As I close this journal of thoughts and remembrances, I should tie up some loose ends for any future readers.

The morning Zeke left, I went out to the barn to feed Molly and muck out her stall. In the bottom of the wheelbarrow, left where I would easily find them, were two shiny objects and a handwritten note. Zeke had left his Medal of Valor to Ma and Nana for taking up arms and defending our home on the night of the shooting and the day Otto barged in. To me he left his deputy sheriff badge, noting that it wasn't a legal appointment, because he had sworn in under his assumed name and not his real one. He wrote that I deserved it more than he did, and he hoped it would always remind me to do what was right. I carry it with me to this day.

When they held the trial for Dave Seegern and Joe Spinks at the county seat, everybody who spoke at the inquest was brought in and put up at the hotel to testify again in court. Seegern was found guilty of murder and sentenced to be hanged, and Spinks was sent to the territorial prison for the rest of his life for aiding in the commission of my pa's murder and for attempting to kill Zeke at our house. We didn't go back for Seegern's execution but were told afterwards that he was dragged, kicking and screaming, to the gallows and had to be tied to a chair over the trap door so the sentence could be carried out.

Ma and Nana never revealed just where Otto got carted off to and buried. I always suspected he was under the manure pile. We kept Otto's horse and rig. The poor animal showed some signs of mistreatment, and we nursed it back to good health. It seemed happy with us. Molly was glad for the company in her waning years.

In the years that followed Zeke Smith's arrival and departure, our little town grew and prospered. Tom Beecher struck a deal with Mr. Schneider to sell his hard cider in the mercantile and did quite well with that business venture. Some folks opened a church and school, both of which I attended and discovered I had a knack, and love, for learning. Ma and Jacob Schneider started keeping company just after he was elected the new town marshal, a job he held for many years without the need for deputies, and they eventually wed. He moved out here with us and proved to be a good and serious man, though I could never feel the same way about him that I did with Pa and Zeke. If he knew that, or sensed it, he never let on and always treated me with love and kindness. I now have a younger half brother and half sister.

Ruth and I grew up together, and I enjoyed her company, though others found her dark and moody. She never did get over the sudden death of her parents. When I went away to the university in Tucson to continue my education, we wrote each other for a while, but she suddenly stopped corresponding with me and moved away.

I became an expert marksman and won several shooting competitions as a youngster and young adult. Thankfully, I have never yet had to shoot another person.

Nana helped Doctor Carne out with his practice for a while as a midwife on house calls and treating minor injuries in his office. We lost her one evening a few years after Zeke left. She was out on the front porch in her rocking chair watching the sunset. As the *last rays of the setting sun faded away, so did she. Ma told me later she was sure she heard Nana say, "Yes, Bryan, I'm ready." We buried her up on the hill next to my pa, and the whole community turned out from miles around to pay their respects. They even took up a collection so we could send away for two inscribed granite headstones for Pa and Nana.*

While in Tucson, with access to newspapers from around the country, I searched countless articles, even though the news was weeks and months old, for any mention of a mysterious stranger who came into the area and helped people with their problems. But I could never find any mention of Zeke Smith or Ezekiel Flagg. I did find out that the little town of Rio Bonita had basically dried up and blown away on the hot South Texas winds.

Now I'm a writer and lecturer in institutions of higher learning. Without getting too personal, I have yet to marry but hope to one day soon. I do hold out hope that Zeke found his lost love and is still out there somewhere helping people in need and setting things right, even though his penance is complete.

ABOUT THE AUTHOR

Rod Timanus has been a writer and illustrator of Old West history throughout his literary career. His history book topics include David Crockett, Lewis and Clark, George Custer, Texas history, and Montezuma Castle and Tuzigoot National Monuments in Arizona. He is a longtime member of the Western Writers of America and has written many WWA convention field trip articles and book reviews for the organization's *Roundup* magazine. He is also a re-enactor with the Arizona Gunfighters, portraying such diverse historical characters as Wild Bill Hickok, Doc Holliday, Curly Bill Brocious, Morgan Earp, and Billy Clanton. At the urging of many friends, and utilizing his historical research knowledge and re-enacting experience, this book is his first foray into the Western fiction genre, with more to follow.

The employees of Thorndike Press hope you have enjoyed this Large Print book. All our Thorndike, Wheeler, and Kennebec Large Print titles are designed for easy reading, and all our books are made to last. Other Thorndike Press Large Print books are available at your library, through selected bookstores, or directly from us.

For information about titles, please call:
(800) 223-1244

or visit our website at:
gale.com/thorndike

To share your comments, please write:
Publisher
Thorndike Press
10 Water St., Suite 310
Waterville, ME 04901